PENGUIN BOOKS

LOVESONG

'Jolley weaves the delicate story of Dalton's fractured life with great care and skill. She makes us want to help him come in from the cold and find the peace he so desperately needs.'

Who Weekly

'*Lovesong* is one of Jolley's finest novels . . . the writing [moves] easily from the bleak to the hilarious, from the black to the deeply touching . . . a passionate exploration of unacceptable yearnings, eroticism and sensuality.'

The Sunday Age

'Elizabeth Jolley has done nothing finer than this touching, quirky tale of memory and loneliness.'

Sydney Morning Herald

'The poetic language and the cornucopia of characters are to be savoured.'

She

'Elizabeth Jolley is dealing here with desires and yearnings so painful, so exquisite, so beyond the pale, that few artists dare frame them in words.'

Australian Book Review

ALSO BY ELIZABETH JOLLEY

Five Acre Virgin and other stories
The Travelling Entertainer and other stories
Palomino
The Newspaper of Claremont Street
Mr Scobie's Riddle
Woman in a Lampshade
Miss Peabody's Inheritance
Foxybaby
Milk and Honey
The Well
The Sugar Mother
My Father's Moon
Cabin Fever
Central Mischief
The Georges' Wife
The Orchard Thieves
Off the Air
Diary of a Weekend Farmer
Fellow Passengers

ELIZABETH
JOLLEY

LOVESONG

PENGUIN BOOKS

Penguin Books Australia Ltd
487 Maroondah Highway, PO Box 257
Ringwood, Victoria, 3134, Australia
Penguin Books Ltd
Harmondsworth, Middlesex, England
Viking Penguin, A Division of Penguin Books USA Inc.
375 Hudson Street, New York, New York 10014, USA
Penguin Books Canada Limited
10 Alcorn Avenue, Toronto, Ontario, Canada, M4V 3B2
Penguin Books (N.Z.) Ltd
Cnr Rosedale and Airborne Roads, Albany, Auckland, New Zealand

First published by Penguin Books Australia Ltd 1997
This edition published by Penguin Books Australia Ltd 1998
1 3 5 7 9 10 8 6 4 2
Copyright © Elizabeth Jolley 1997

Designed by Jo Hunt, Penguin design studio
Illustration of park bench by Michelle Ryan
Typeset in 12.25/17 Centaur by Midland Typesetters, Maryborough, Victoria
Made and printed in Australia by Australian Print Group, Maryborough Victoria

National Library of Australia
Cataloguing-in-Publication data:

Jolley, Elizabeth, 1923–
Lovesong.

ISBN 014 0272755

I. Title.

A823.3

I would like to express my thanks to the Curtin University of Technology for the continuing privilege of being with students and colleagues in the School of Communication and Cultural Studies and for the provision of a room in which to write. I would like, in particular, to thank Don Watts, Peter Reeves, Brian Dibble, Barbara Milech, Ian Reid, Anne Brewster and Don Grant. In addition I would like to thank John Maloney, John de Laeter, Don Yeats, Ross Bennett and Tony Nicholls.

A special thanks is offered to Nancy McKenzie who, for a great many years, has typed my manuscripts. She is endlessly patient.

I would like as well to thank Kay Ronai, an especially thoughtful and sensitive editor. And I would like to thank Bruce Sims and Caroline Lurie for their advice and encouragement.

In addition, I would like to thank all those people at Penguin Books Australia who work so hard to produce and market the finished books.

ACKNOWLEDGEMENTS

Earlier versions of some sections have been previously published as:

'The Grass House' (from a work in progress) in *Memory: Southerly 3*, edited by Ivor Indyk and Elizabeth Webby, HarperCollins, North Ryde, 1991.

'The Halfway House' in *Millennium: Time-Pieces by Australian Writers*, edited by Helen Daniel, Penguin Books, Ringwood, 1991.

'Motel Marriage' in *Femmes de Siècle: Stories from the 90s: Women Writing at the End of Two Centuries*, edited by Joan Smith, Chatto and Windus, London, 1992.

The author wishes to acknowledge the use of Wilhelm Müller's 'Der Greise Kopf' from *Winterreise, 14 Song Cycle*, and extracts from R. M. Rilke's 'Liebeslied' and 'The Panther', and W. B. Yeats' 'Song of the Wandering Aengus'.

'Fiction is ... the response to a deep
and always hidden wound.'

FLAUBERT

LIEBESLIED (Love Song)

Wie soll ich meine Seele halten, dass
sie nicht an deine rührt?...
Doch alles, was uns anrührt, dich und mich,
nimmt uns zusammen wie ein Bogenstrich,
der aus zwei Saiten eine Stimme zieht.

Auf welches Instrument sind wir gespannt?...
O süsses Lied.

How could I keep my soul so that it might
not touch on yours?...
Yet all that touches us, myself and you,
takes us together like a violin bow
that draws a single voice out of two strings.

Upon what instrument have we been strung?...
Sweet is the song.

R. M. RILKE

Sometimes during concerts he thought that, in the expression in the eyes of the conductor, he could see the reflection of the exquisite moment of perfection and of satisfaction achieved privately between the conductor and the musician concerned in the performance of the particular little phrase in the music. Especially this was so when the little phrase was played by itself and then, with matching notes, perhaps from the piano. For example, the pianist in musical communication with the flautist, the conductor, watchful, leading them together in readiness for the awaited satisfying invasion of the whole orchestra which would bring about the ultimate, the climax.

The movement of the shoulders, the head and the delicate hands – the whole body of the conductor involved completely with the creation of the music, together with the penetrating gaze of concentration, would bring about the awaited desired result and immediately soften the sharp glance to a caressing look of tenderness and deference. A look which was full of admiration and respect, a perfect understanding of love and gratitude passing between conductor and musician. The whole ensemble, then, breaking the precarious silent homage to the moment, would, with their energy and restrained precision, enter the performance once more.

He is, of course, excluded from all this as he no longer takes part (singing) and, in any case, does not go to concerts. He simply has the music in his heart and his mind.

To begin with at the time in Cambridge he had no idea whether he was accused or not. He did not know if he was being blamed. It seemed impossible that he should be. Blamed, that is, from outside. He thought he might be accused even if the anticipated harm was merely in himself and had not been laid upon someone else, for instance, the child. He already knew, at the time, though was unable to explain anything, what was within himself, and it was this that led him to think of and imagine the gossip passing between unimaginable people, his tutors, his professor even, his fellows and their friends and their visitors – in neighbouring colleges – even the persons who made his bed and cleaned his room surely, with knowing glances, whispered. They all blamed him, he thought for something they might, in fact, have done themselves to harm themselves; all overlooking that now known and intrinsic fact that the qualities of type and the path which is the individual's destiny are shared out and present in the newly born, and are well defined and developed in the first few weeks of life, thus shaping the actual kind of life each will have. Needs and environment affect each one differently and the effects are shaped long before they are shown.

Straight away he was haunted by the loneliness which accompanies fear and which lies hidden in the heart and from which no words can pass the lips. And so, without the relief of speech, this silence persisted and finding himself unable to continue, he dealt with the matter in the only way he knew.

During his solitary walking now to the house and to the park and back to Mrs Porter's he thinks of the particular time and the particular incident repeatedly arranging, in his mind, ways in which the whole experience could be relived, brought forward and refashioned so that everything would be different, leaving an entirely satisfactory and happy reflection, in other words, a stored consolation.

He remembers his scorn for his own father and his own inability, his refusal perhaps, to see through his father's jovial hopefulness and his eager ways with trade, to knowing really that he (his father) was deeply sad and that he never allowed himself to reveal this sadness to anyone.

His father was a lean man, spare, but not with the elegance, the aristocratic slenderness, so wished for by his mother and his aunt. His father was lean from hungry poverty in his childhood; not an intentional mean upbringing, but simply he was from a poor household. The aunt, his father's sister, had contrived to submerge any hint of this undesirable background in a wealth of richness in her language, in her laughter and in her way of being with his mother.

Sometimes when he walks he replaces these thoughts with imaginary pictures of the little girl, the child he hopes to find, crying alone in her bed. In these imagined scenes he sees himself leaning over, kneeling at the small bedside, begging her not to cry, telling her that he is with her and that she will sleep safely because he is watching over her. So consoling and faithful is this image that he stops walking and stands still in the dark silence under the trees, the only sound being a cracking twig when he resumes his walking.

Vom Abendrot zum Morgenlicht
Ward mancher Kopf zum Greise
Wer glaubt's? Und meiner ward es nicht
Auf dieser ganzen Reise.

Between dusk and dawn many a head has turned
White. Who can believe it? And mine has not
changed on all this long journey.

'Der Greise Kopf', *Winterreise*
WILHELM MÜLLER 1794-1827

'Where did you find us?' Dalton Foster asked aunt Dalton. 'Where did you find mother and me?'

'You? Where did I find your beloved mamma and where did I find you?' Aunt Dalton put down her pretty hair brush and, hugging him, became conspiratorial. 'You, you wicked little wretch, were hidden inside your mamma. You, you were a surprise, a little surprise and then a big surprise and I,' she went on, 'I was *hiding* and I jumped out on your mamma. I was *her* surprise.'

'Merton? Merton? Who is this Merton?' Dalton heard his mother's voice, angry and tearful, hysterical with discovery.

'Miss Merton,' aunt Dalton said with emphasis on the Miss. 'Miss Merton, someone,' she said. 'You don't even know.'

That aunt Dalton could have a preferred Friend was a shock to Dalton and he felt his mother's pain.

Somehow the magic of the summer-house with the warm smell of dust and the lazy spider on the tilted floor was a consolation later when he sat beside aunt Dalton at the little round table, drawing flowers with coloured pencils.

'Now a red one,' aunt Dalton said, 'and now a blue

7

one, and now which colour would you like to choose?'

The flowers, when aunt Dalton was drawing them, had tiny faces. Dalton chose green for his flower.

'But Darling Child!' aunt Dalton said, 'the stalks and leaves will be green, so choose a colour.' Dalton chose black and aunt Dalton sighed. 'Now another red one,' she said, 'and now a blue one.'

They were interrupted by Rose coming from the tall London house across the cut grass of the lawn. Rose, in her white apron and seeming to bring with her the muted sounds of the city, admired the drawings and told aunt Dalton that yes she had taken a tray upstairs and that she, aunt Dalton, was required to be up those very stairs. Aunt Dalton jumped up immediately.

'My Precious Child, I shall not be long,' she said to Dalton, 'make some more flowers for me,' and she was gone, her feet scarcely touching the soft grass. Rose, more slowly, followed her.

The summer-house creaked and there was only the sloping floor to consider. Dalton, lazy like the spider in the summer warmth, tried to think of Christmas. Aunt Dalton had spoken of painting and a new paint box he might receive. He thought of the colours she had named. The box would be made up of little white squares and in these squares there would be the new clean colours. White and black, of course, and then the mysterious names, ultramarine, prussian blue, cobalt blue, orange and yellow, ordinary names like brown, purple and green, and then there would be yellow ochre, burnt sienna, vermilion, crimson lake, rose madder ... rose madder.

'Rose,' he jumped up and ran after her. 'Rose! rose madder,' he shouted.

Rose. Rose? Well, Rose came and went, depending on whether the accommodation supplied required her. Now, if it was a hotel there was no need for Rose. But a house, *that* was different ...

Often when Dalton Foster is walking alone, and he walks alone a great deal, he has no recollection now of anything following the disturbed serenity of the paper-flower faces in the summer-house. And the name, the name of Merton, Miss Merton, never being mentioned again, in spite of her powerful and brief intrusion, disappearing for ever.

As he walks, Dalton, with the more finished and complete memories, sometimes feels he has, all at once, a profound vision which gives him an identity. He, at these times which are not frequent, has a sense of having a past and a presence in the present. Without wanting to, he understands that he might be forced, sooner than expected, to acknowledge a future which, during this present time in his life, is not heralded, either wisely or foolishly by the possibility of any change for the better.

Sometimes the mysterious edges of a profound vision can be nebulous like the name of Merton or the remembered rough-fringed bandage falling over his eyes, long ago, without any memory of the reason for it being there. Or there could be a series of half-remembered, small acts hidden in the deep green of a garden at dusk or, in dappled images, caught in a haze of sunlight pouring through the purple and gold of stained glass, the dust-filled shaft of light seeming to rest with forgiving tenderness on the fair, almost white, curls of a child.

Mrs Porter's Establishment. Guest House, the Station road end of the city, near railway line and derelict factory. Pub on first corner west. Mrs Porter: Landlady (widowed) Business woman and Agent. Owns Large Old House, really 2 houses, one behind the other. 3 Floors (in places). Furnishing minimal. 1 connecting Bathroom and Toilet. Private Bathroom position not revealed. Dining Room. Cold.

Miss Emily Vales. EV for short. Typiste (indifferent) but a whiz at baby-sitting. Renowned for foiling, single handed, an intruder intent on kidnapping the 5 year old violinist prodigy, son of Dr and Mrs Barnett; 'Lovely People' in Miss Vales' very own words. Ambition: 'I'm waiting for Mr Right.' Clothes: Peter Pan collars, ankle sox, fake jewellery, blouses, mainly pink and yellow. Favourite perfume: Jasmine.

Mrs Disley: Mrs Porter's maid, personal daily woman. Does breakfasts 12 noon for the 3 young men in the entertainment line, upstairs back. Interests: Graffiti. Ambition: None, 'Gave it away' (own words).

The three young gentlemen, Pootsie, Trotter and Slem. Into Drag. Dancers. 12 noon breakfasts – on trays (Mrs Disley). Ambition: Drag.

Guest House Meals: None, except for light breakfast daily in dining room 7.30 a.m. Only resident guests, named on this page, eligible for evening meal.

There are other Lodgers, some named and some simply grey shapes in the front hall, on the stairs and passing in and out of partly open doors.

Mr Porter: deceased, referred to briefly.

Mrs Porter is pouring tea.

'Well, as I've tode joo before when Mr Porter looked out the window and saw the car parked right outside the window up on the footpath it was prackerly in my front room, where Miss Whatsaname is, well ... *there*, he said *not in this house not under this roof* and I said to him, there and then I said, it's orl right Mr P I tode you, he's just sleeping over that's all and he said *sleeping over?* Sleeping *here* in this house *with my daughter!* He had this daughter didjoo know from his first wife, what's wrong he wanted to know then with the back seat of the car — that's what he wanted to know and he started up the top stairs would joo believe and I said it's a bit late now Mr P and isn't it time you was orf down the hotel. And if you don't mind I tode him it is *my* house and *my* roof and as I said as sure as I am sitting here with this tea pot that was the last thing I said. Mr P, I said, it's a bit late now isn't it time you went and bowled he was at the corner there just married a week. Sylvie moved out. No reason for her to stay on here with her daddy run over dead and buried. She had the car and I said just you pack your stuff and take your young man so she did and orf she went. The minx.

'That's Mr Porter's hair ball,' Mrs Porter, noticing Dalton Foster's quick sideways glance, said. 'I keep it under that bell glass on there on the mantel. A reminder. Been there ever since Mr Porter passed on. All of thirty years.' She flicked what was supposed to pass for a tear from somewhere near her eye but not too far from her other hand from which she was counting notes, Mr Dalton Foster's key money and four weeks' rent in advance. During Mrs Porter's absence in search of a spare key there was time for a closer scrutiny of the unusual ornament. It appeared to have been sliced in half, perhaps with a corrugated bread-knife, he thought then.

He thinks now, without wanting to, of all the colours pressed into a curious pattern, black and grey and brown, layered and speckled with a reddish auburn and a white of the off-white sort. A generously brindled record, as it turned out, of forty years of hairdressing. Men and Boys. 'Would never keep his mouth shut. Always had the time of day for his customers. Not that it was the barbering as took him,' Mrs Porter assured Mr Foster. 'A bus bowled him on the corner, by the hotel, just down the road,' she explained. 'Married a week,' she said. 'Mown down, he was, and dead on arrival as they say.'

Mr Foster, reflecting, feels that Mrs Porter had been well pleased with the turn of events.

❧

Mr Dalton Foster, standing cautiously after his first night, on the threshold of a new life, in his doorway, on the first floor, hearing *Viennese Delights* on compact disc in a radio request programme, pauses and listens to the music, muffled by distance and the baize-covered door at the end of the hall downstairs. This door, which is always kept closed, closes over the entrance to the back part of the house which is in reality like a second house behind the first which is, in Mrs Porter's words, on the street. The second house is exclusively Mrs Porter's region and is a place for the more exclusive paying guests. Also, the kitchen is there.

The house is not thought of as a house of music, though the previous evening Mr Foster had heard, for a short time, the subdued and flat piano notes from Miss Mallow's room (downstairs front), the room immediately below his room. But that could hardly be called music. The *Viennese Delights* unexpectedly recall for Mr Foster his aunt Dalton's regrettable habit of listening, during the war, to forbidden wireless programmes. She listened, saying then that she was quite agreeable to regard the hideous atmospherics, the fadings, the silences and the sudden return of grotesque exaggerated sound as a punishment for her vice. She did not hide her listenings to the news in German and the unflattering comments about the British and the British colonies. These comments were uttered unmistakably by a traitor who was also a spy. Such listening was not at all suitable for the sister of a Consul even if the Consul, Dalton Foster senior, was purely a representative for trade. Trade, young Dalton's mother and aunt lamented and sighed with the regret of it. They both so desired art and culture but Dalton T. (T for Trade, as they called him to distinguish the father from the son) was so incurably cut out, even in the way his ears protruded, for trade. Trade – wool, wheat, timber, oils, machinery parts, even letter paper and envelopes and bandages – nothing was too big or too small.

I mean, where can we go to meet sculptors and musicians and authors, the two women would have wept but instead, whenever they could, they organized little dinner parties mixing musicians and art gallery directors with factory floor managers and ships' chandlers.

'What is a Consul?' little Dalton had asked his mother once. She seemed to ponder the question.

'Your father,' and then, consumed with mirth, she

had been unable to go on. He had looked it up in his school dictionary.

Either of two annual highest officers of the ancient Roman republic (first c., title of Napoleon in French Republic 1799–1804); State agent residing in foreign town ... His father, obviously, went back a long way.

Sometimes his mother called his father 'Foster', declaring it was a quaint European custom, really continental. German and Austrian women, in particular, called their husbands by their surnames. It was appealing. Very chic.

Dalton Foster, still lingering in his doorway, straightens his tie and, wondering why his mother and aunt Dalton should come, all at once, into his mind, goes downstairs in search of the dining room and breakfast. He has not thought of his mother or aunt Dalton for some time. Perhaps the memories are a part of the experience of coming back into the community after working meticulously for half his life through a sentence and a cure in various special institutions. Voluntarily, as if to put off this emergence, the cure was undertaken several times.

The last time he saw aunt Dalton she was sitting up close to a horrible little plastic table banging a dish with a spoon and wearing a bib decorated with provocative slogans. The visit, arranged for compassionate reasons, had upset Dalton. Weeping in the van on the return

16

journey he realised how she, aunt Dalton, would have hated the cheapness of the little table if she had realised she was sitting at it. Seeking consolation he read that night;

There are times of righteousness and justice and we live in a time of righteousness and revelation

(*Revelations* XX 4)

and he thought then that, instead of being where he was, he should be at his desk somewhere, looking up quotations to enhance what he wanted to write.

On this first morning at Mrs Porter's, Mr Foster starts on the socks knitted for him by his mother and aunt Dalton against the time when he would be on his own.

Against his old age. They had laughed when they had given him the socks, as if old age was an impossibility for him. He is not yet what he considers to be old or even elderly and was lately surprised in a bus, his first bus journey for several years, when two youths were addressed as if through a megaphone; 'On your feet youse! Stand up willya and give the old gent here a go.'

'I mean mixed toilets. I arsk you! All this unisex, where does it get you? Did joo know it's a known fact, a medical known fact, as men can't pass water if they can hear a woman passing water ...? It was on that particular bus journey, when he was seated in the unwillingly relinquished place, that one of the two middle-aged ladies sitting directly behind him made this startling observation. Another indication, he realised then, that like his suit, he was out of date.

Dalton Foster is glad to have the socks. He is missing his early tea. He is ashamed to realise how important his first cup of tea is to him. He feels this sort of thing should not matter but he has to acknowledge his disappointment with the lukewarm milky liquid which Mrs Porter, her large arm outstretched, hands him. Mrs Porter, he notices, keeps the tea pot snuggled beside her and, whenever she pours a cup of tea for another arrival at breakfast, she tops up her own. The fullness of the top part of Mrs Porter's body seems to rest on the table.

Breakfast, which had seemed an important part of the day ahead of him, is over very quickly. Mrs Porter explains afresh to each guest in turn, as she hands the allowed one cup, that she is obliged to drop the breakfast egg, what with rates and taxes going up the way they are. Breakfast is suddenly small, hardly anything of an event, all over by a quarter past eight. Mr Foster is still hungry. He understands too that the dining room which he is being asked to leave is cold and that his own room, to which he should retreat, is even colder. Mrs Porter, in another explanation for him alone, since the others know, says that guests cannot remain at the table as the maid wants to clear and get done.

In the hall at the foot of the stairs Mr Foster has to catch a sneeze in his handkerchief. He has a cold coming on. He can sense in himself the particular loss of balance in outlook which a threatened head cold can bring about. He always does catch cold in a new environment.

'The darling disadvantaged child,' aunt Dalton sympathised repeatedly, in hotel bedrooms, all across Europe when he sat with streaming eyes and his throat too sore to swallow the fragrant croissant torn up by his aunt's nimble fingers and offered to him, coffee soaked, steaming on a spoon.

'I have a piano in my room.' Miss Mallow, waiting till Mr Foster has raised his face from his handkerchief, introduces herself. 'I have a piano pupil who comes.' She pauses, with a glance at the stained glass of the front door. Mr Foster fingers his chin and nods.

'I'm looking for a position,' Miss Mallow explains, her vague expression becoming strained. 'I have a reference,' she says, 'if you should happen to hear of something.' Mr Foster gives another of his small nods. Miss Mallow pulls a folded sheet of very thin notepaper from her cardigan pocket. 'Here it is,' she says. 'Mr Afton wrote it for me.' Mr Foster reads the page because he thinks he ought to.

'A reference, a testimonial,' Miss Mallow says in a low voice. 'I'm very fortunate that Mr Afton, he was my Headmaster, d'you see, I am fortunate that he was able to ... You can never tell, can you, in advance, how your life and your circumstances can change.'

Mr Foster sees that the thin spidery handwriting goes off the edge of the page so that some words are only half there. The old-fashioned phrases, he supposes with his lately realized lack of knowledge, will be of very little use in present-day requirements for a teaching post or for getting work of any kind. He hands it back to Miss Mallow. On Mrs Porter's hall clock it is barely eight-twenty.

'There are two of us,' the young man on the stairs tells Mr Foster. 'We are in the room next to yours. You and us,' he says, 'are up front in this house. You and the two of us.' They were not dancers, he makes it clear, not like the boys upstairs at the back. 'There's these three pretty boys upstairs back, such pretty boys,' he insists, 'with gold heads, rosy cheeks and cherry-red lips and, of course, their ear-rings.' These three, he explains, are something in the entertainment line, a floor show at the hotel, that sort of thing. 'But not us,' the young man, the taller of the two, changes his tone. They are standing, all three, wedged on the stairs.

'There's something wrong with both of us,' the taller young man continues. 'I'm a waiter,' he says. 'I've been tested positive. I've got TB also, through no fault of my own but who'll ever believe that. People keep telling me, "How thin and pale you are!" It's true,' he sighs, 'regrettably true. My blue suit simply *hangs* on me especially when I try to stand up straight. And Perce here, Sgt Major Perce, you'll never believe this but he's getting a bust. He says it's painful under his uniform, under the double buttons, see? Looks as if he's got a cushion stuffed in under his tunic. Take a look at that chest! Awkward, isn't it? He's the door man at the hotel. Awkward for him to have a bust. Night times we do a bit of baby-sitting depending on our shifts. The two of us. Mrs Porter's agency, see. The baby-sitting. Helps out with the rent. It's like this,' he lowers his voice, 'Mrs Porter likes to make double use.' He pauses. Mr Foster questions the remark by raising his eyebrows.

The two men stand aside as much as it is possible to stand aside on a staircase, and Mr Foster goes on up slowly, stepping carefully on the worn-out carpet. He reflects that not only had he not known what to say to the young men, he also had not noticed before how thin the stair carpet is. At the turn of the stairs, from the first landing, he looks down to the young men, who have reached the hall, and gives them the smallest wave, a slight flap of the hand, a small sign from his shy heart.

The carpet in Mr Foster's room is worn out too. He supposes, as he looks at it, that this is what threadbare means, the private, pale, woven threads belonging to the birth of the carpet for anyone to look at.

At the rehabilitation centre there were no carpets and some rooms did not have windows. He thinks of this room as being windowless. This is not strictly true. He knows there are windows, there is a little row of them high up. At night they give the impression of being small and barred, like windows in a prison or in the special locked part of a special hospital. The street lamps, providing a weak night-light during the wakeful first night, caused the shadows of the thin window frames to make a pattern of bars on the opposite wall.

Standing uncertainly in the middle of his room with the door closed, Mr Foster listens for the sounds of the two young men, the infected waiter and the deformed door man, coming up to their room. He feels ashamed that he minds so much about his tea. He has never, in all his worst experiences, had tea as bad as the tea Mrs

Porter had poured for him. He wishes now for a pot of tea, a whole pot to himself. He understood during his first meeting with Mrs Porter, who said, he must understand, that everything he wanted he would have at her guest house and yes, whole pots of tea, one per person, were the norm in her establishment.

He continues to wait in his cold room in the hope of hearing something which would indicate that the bathroom was unoccupied. During the night he had been amazed at himself not asking to see the bathroom before paying in advance a considerable sum for key money and four weeks' rent. The bathroom, which Mrs Porter had declared herself to be madly in love with, and completely unable to part with for something more modern (she adored, she said, her brass taps) was, in one plain word, appalling. The more so because there was only one. To forgive himself for his unforgivable oversight he consoled himself with one of his more comfortable images that of the hotel bedroom where his aunt Dalton would say to his mother for goodness sake to take the little wretch out – somewhere nice and out of sight – as she herself had every intention of retiring for the whole afternoon with a book. Often during the many bleak years of his life he had returned, in his mind, to this image of aunt Dalton stretched out gracefully reading in the comfortable room which had the additional luxury of a bright fire, lit specially by the devoted *femme de chambre* at his aunt's request.

Still standing in his room he tries to recall the names of the other guests present at breakfast. There was hardly enough toast to go round, less than was offered at his boarding school, years ago, and certainly lacking the therapeutic, but unimaginative, generosity of foods provided at his recent place of residence.

Perhaps, because of his presence, a new guest, at the breakfast table, there was considerable animated conversation. An Emily Vales recounted, at length, an experience already known to the assembled company. Mrs Porter prompted Miss Vales at intervals. This gave Mrs Porter the appearance of a modest benevolence in spite of which the meal, not augmented with more toast, was over very quickly.

Alone in his cold room it is not difficult for Dalton to imagine his mother and aunt Dalton recreating, as was their way, this Miss Vales and her night of heroism. To begin with, they would regard her as 'that cheap little shop assistant', despising her vulgar clothes and ornaments. They would see unmistakable signs of advancing age; 'rising forty' (Dalton's mother). 'No, darling,' from aunt Dalton, 'utterly the wrong side of forty, if she's a day.' Both women would be changing voice, speech and expression to appear as if they belonged to the uneducated lower classes. They would describe in the breathless idiom of the ignorant and stupid how she, the baby-sitter, was sitting in her especially made bed at the doctor's house, surrounded by magazines and chocolates *and* the TV *wheeled in on purpose*, when she had seen, *with her own eyes*, the rough leg of the intruder cocked and coming stealthily over the balcony, knocking over a metal chair and breaking pot plants.

'I never thought I'd see blood all over the little bathroom.' Aunt Dalton would manage a whine and a sniff in imitation of Miss Vales. 'I reelly reelly thought it was Mr Right come at last ...'

'And the gun, don't, do not forget the gun on the piano downstairs,' Dalton's mother would contribute to the recounting of the story, adding Mrs Porter's announcement that Mr Right is not far away, for every pot there is a lid, Mr Right might well be waiting for Miss Vales around the very next corner.

Dalton recalls the events easily. Red hair, a limp and a squint, someone to be avoided, an intruder partly disguised with a cardigan over his head.

'You should never have cut peep holes in that lovely cable stitch,' Miss Vales had reported her reprimand, while telling of her night of fear during which, with presence of mind, she had stuffed the intruder with apple pie, vodka and orange, *and* port and lemon *and*, flattering him, had danced all along the picture gallery, at gun point, while the child slept on upstairs, safe and undisturbed in his pretty night-nursery.

'Picture gallery?' Dalton's mother questions.

'Of course, darling,' Aunt Dalton reminds, 'the parvenu, the *nouveau riche*, they have libraries, music rooms, newly appointed kitchens and bathrooms and, of course, galleries and conservatories. There is also a price on their children either in the form of kidnapping or of blackmail. Our brave little baby-sitter should have her picture in the newspaper for foiling single-handed the intentions of a bad man.'

'That's right,' Dalton's mother, in her newly acquired voice, replies, 'we play and dance and eat and sing and drink and then he slips in the kiddy's bathroom, splitting his head on the porcelain, and bleeds to death.'

'Don't you forget,' aunt Dalton reminds, 'our heroine has described herself tied up with a filthy rope. She has to wait till the morning, attached to a balcony chair, till the doctor and his wife return from their slumber party. Picture it, aunt Dalton laughs in adenoidal tones, 'the wealthy *Kings and Queens of Insomnia*, a willing Sheherazade in attendance, endlessly telling and embellishing . . .'

⁂

Hoping that the bathroom is now free, Dalton leaves his room, recalling for himself the description, surprisingly vivid, of the doctor and his knowledge of *the secret places in the human body which, when pressed hard, caused intense pain and immediate death*. All this, he understands is stored in Miss Vales. She used this knowledge to threaten the intruder, to frighten him, to try to make him leave before the doctor and his violent temper and superhuman strength returned; ... *being a doctor he knows the human body and can press all the fatal places and kill in seconds ... he killed an intruder, in a fit of temper, at a party once ...*

Anyone who is not wanted in a particular place can be regarded as an intruder. Dalton understands this truth. He seems to hear, in his head, Miss Vales talking, her voice rising as if questioning at the end of every phrase. She would have known then, at that time, that similarly her own body, as well as that of someone else, might be if, *in the way*, subject to this quick and painful method of disposal.

As he combs his hair, Dalton, seeing his own starved reflection in the bathroom mirror, can imagine the quick and anxious glance with which Miss Vales would prepare to leave the house every day. He recalls, without wanting to, that when leaving the breakfast table earlier, he, without meaning to, momentarily stands aside to let Miss Vales go first.

In this small action there is this tiny pause which aunt Dalton calls *toujours la politesse*, and Dalton is compelled, unwillingly, to catch the strained look on Miss Vales' face. The expression in her eyes reveals suddenly and unexpectedly a depth of sorrow which, if he is honest, he understands could be a reflection of the hungry expression in his own eyes. Her face, which might be pretty when animated, gives an impression of youth but in reality is lined, laden is perhaps a better word, with the experience of unrewarded living, the endless sorrow of having failed to be chosen. The moment of confrontation passes but the pleading eyes haunt him. His own eyes fill with tears, there in front of the blemished mirror. He drops the comb and putting both hands over his face, his chest about to burst, he sobs in a silent anguish for something he is not able to bear. Perhaps something, in a calmer frame of mind, he would think of as the 'pain of the world' and would then put it on one side, after writing it down somewhere in a note book.

Someone is, with impatience, knocking and rattling the handle of the bathroom door. He, with a quick movement, wipes his face on his towel and picks up his comb.

⌘

Very much earlier in the morning it seemed to Mr Foster that he saw a stork fly past the little row of high-up windows. The heavy bird filled the small patches of sky and disappeared.

Out in the street he sets off for what feels like a compulsory walk. He looks up at the chimney stacks and at the various crazy roof tops, trying to see if a stork could be standing up there, on one leg, half hidden by brickwork and rusted corrugated iron.

He wishes for a stork. He wishes for some creature beyond his reach which could be watched and wondered about. Glimpses, on certain days, of the bird would furnish him with a sort of romantic hope. He would be on the edge once more of something exotic, some other possibility in life like the time when aunt Dalton told him that she was unable to be unexcited when she heard a contralto and a soprano together in a duet. Counter tenor and boy soprano, she had said then softly in his ear, had the same effect. A superb unravelling of something inside, she confessed. A confession, she said laughing, a feeling of ecstasy, of perfection, the innocent boyish voice in harmony with the specially developed tenor of the mature singer who has taught himself to surrender and, at the same time, to exercise complete control while singing in this double harmony of question and reply. Bach, aunt Dalton said then, had a perfect understanding of human timing, wish and hearing. On the same day his mother had confided that she could not bear the sound of her husband (Mr Foster's father) sneezing. Trying to explain this to herself, she said she had come up with the idea that the sound of his sneeze was a reminder of his existence.

The stork, Mr Foster is sure, if it were possible for one to exist nearby, would make certain days special. He knows, though, that he will not, in his small wanderings, see a stork.

Somewhere far off there is the sound of the long drawn-out melancholy cry from a train approaching the level crossings. The horn cries and the sullen rumblings of the empty wheat wagons follow the horn. Later, the whole long train will pass behind the fence on the other side of the road opposite Mrs Porter's place and will continue, accompanied by narrow country roads and the faithful water pipes, far across distant paddocks.

Somewhere close by, within him, the remembered music overflows. The question and the reply, the boy soprano and the ardent but controlled tenor, described in aunt Dalton's passionate whisper, causing a shiver to pass through him was, in other words, the alternation of acceptance and denial.

Mr Foster crosses the road, feeling the cold wind from the east at his back.

Mrs Porter pours tea and reads the paper.

HOME OWNER CLEARED OF PICK-AXE

There's too many cleared. Only last week there was that mugging in the car park it was right by the supermarket you'd think you was safe right by there wouldn't you well she never let go her hand bag dragged to her death she was and *He was cleared*.

I've ordered-in *Chinese*. There's duck and plum sauce, brockly, fried rice and a beef dish with chilli. Mrs Porter puts down the paper.

Mrs Porter tells Miss Vales not to have the beef, you'll be up all night EV, that's what chilli does.

Mrs Porter's establishment is close to the city, close to transport, one foot practically in the park and the other in the shopping mall to say nothing else the pub's handy too.

We don't ask no questions. Mrs Porter maintains her place is a Home from Home for Homeless Gentlemen.

Mrs Porter, on re-reading Miss Vales' palm and her tea leaves, predicts *a stranger has come to town and is just around the corner*.

A Mr Dalton Foster (not eligible for the *Chinese*) he's only settled for breakfast and will be at that meal. Miss Vales will be seeing Mr Right as soon as tomorrow ...

Waste paper, hamburger wrappings, soft-drink containers and other more intimate rubbish, reminders of human nocturnal activities, seem to collect in the street outside Mrs Porter's establishment and along the tufted grass where a cyclone-wire fence prevents the careless walker from suiciding on the railway lines opposite. Immediately in front of the house is a lamp post and a tree which has been neatly trimmed, some would say severely lopped, because of the overhead electricity wires.

Mr Dalton Foster notices that Miss Mallow has the tree by her window. He envies her the window and the rough, sometimes sun-patterned bark of the tree.

Next door, on the same side of the street, there is another lodging house, the real thing, a half-way hostel for people discharged from special hospitals and institutions. Outside, a small group of these people are waiting for their transport, a special bus which takes them to their work. Mostly, Mrs Porter told Dalton at breakfast, they go to a place where they fold cardboard into boxes. Mrs Porter's inflexion on the word 'they' set them aside, once and for all, as being inmates rather than paying guests as in her own house. In spite of the cold morning they, these set-aside people, are still in cotton clothes. A few have on something thinly woollen, a cardigan or a jacket, pulled tight across the chest. The mist hanging damp over the waste land beside the railway shows no sign of dispersing. The people stand close together. No one looks up as he passes. They seem, as he goes by, to study the ground even more closely. He thinks of the people recently met in Mrs Porter's house: the infected waiter and his companion, the door man with his unfortunate deformity: Miss Mallow, an elderly and forlorn piano teacher, as lonely and as cold as Dalton himself. There are others he has not seen yet, there are the boys described as being in the entertainment line. They sleep 'upstairs back' and keep late hours. They are dancers with rouged lips and cheeks, curled hair, ear-rings and handbags. Then there are others, vague greyish men and women inhabiting the other parts of the house. These people slip along the passage and disappear, as if furtively, through the baize-covered door at the end of the passage on the ground floor. If Dalton Foster thinks of all these people, and especially if he considers himself, there is only a small amount of money which makes the difference, the small difference, between those lodging in Mrs Porter's place and the people, on the footpath, shivering while they wait for their special bus.

Dalton, in his isolation, studies as he passes, a torn poster describing a film; *a criminal on the run from the police*

returns to the scenes of his childhood and continues to commit offences
... Most of the posters, on the stained wall, have been partly removed or spoiled in some way.

Ahead of him, on the road, is a man who is clearly destitute. He is walking in the gutter. His long hair clings to his head and neck. He looks as if he has spent the whole night in the rain. He carries a heavy bag. All he possesses, Dalton thinks, and he envies the man for being unable to be more destitute and, because of this, has some form of rescue ahead. Dalton Foster's respectability and his just above inadequate means prevent him from any kind of rescue; the warm bed, the hot tea — even if it is in a tin mug, and the lifting of all responsibility which is a part of being in a shelter for the destitute.

He walks on, crossing the invisible boundary between the derelict edge of the city and the ancient residential suburb which he had known as a boy, and which was now undergoing the changes from quiet substantial houses, surrounded by trees and lawns and flowers, to consulting rooms for doctors and tall blocks of offices for all other kinds of consultations, chiefly, he suspects, to do with money. The new buildings do not match at all with the existing older ones and this produces an unforgivable uneasiness. As he passes the hotel, the scene of Mr Porter's unregretted demise many years ago, he is startled by an invitation in coloured chalk on a small blackboard to a:

Gentlemen Only Raunchy Lunch Lingerie and See Through Bar Bunnies Thursdays only. Floor Show Nude Every Nite

He has to understand, yet again, that he has emerged, surfaced perhaps, in an unfamiliar world. Glancing back from the hotel corner he is surprised to see how large Mrs Porter's house is. Double storeyed, it looks as though two houses have been built together to make one. He supposes the houses, Mrs Porter's place and the half-way hostel, are on what is called desirable land. He imagines both buildings being demolished by an enormous iron ball swinging from a crane or being blown up, imploded from inside, and then systematically sorted and stacked, the bricks and timber sold as salvage. A skyscraper of offices, doomed to lack of use, would replace the rubble and, in the light of the setting sun, the innumerable windows would glow as if made of thin but durable layers of gold.

ço

'If you cry on your birthday,' aunt Dalton said from the recesses of a feather bed, to Dalton's mother, 'you'll cry all the year round.' His mother said she knew that and hadn't she cried all year, last year and the year before last year and all the year before that?

'Rubbish,' aunt Dalton said and reminded her of the consular dinner given, *for once*, for a visiting Arts Council officer, where she had laughed immodestly and for a long time and where, to start off with, she had insisted on cough mixture for a pre-dinner drink, grudgingly settling for whisky in the absence of something made by Vicks. In their remembering, both women collapsed in what they, in artificial voices, their lips pursed, called unseemly laughter. They stopped laughing immediately when Dalton's father came into the room. Sometimes then it seemed to Dalton that his mother and his aunt were married, thus causing his father to seem to be more of an uncle. There was in particular a memory, a recollection of being in a dark leafy garden at dusk, the trodden grass damp and fragrant, and the two women dressed as if for a party or a wedding, smiling with their arms round each other and his father, dark in shade, sombre at nightfall, as if out of focus, on the edge looking like an intruder either trying to be included in the merriment or to make an escape from it. Dalton remembers himself lying in the roots of the hedge trying then not to move in case a twig should snap. Later indoors, after his father had left, aunt Dalton tumbled shrieking on the blue silk of the rented Regency sofa. Did you hear, she managed at last. Did you hear *The Archduke* at the wrong speed all through the soup!

It is an evening which Dalton Foster remembers very well, particularly as he walks towards the street where now, years later, he will be visiting the house which is still very much the same as it was. It is a tall solid house, airless with bunched curtains and with matching frills on chairs and sofas. A house draped with too much material, from ceiling to floor, at knee level and eye level and in between all levels. Choked in curtains and cushions, he remembers that he was included then in the evening, being considered at twelve to be just old enough.

Pumpkin soup, aunt Dalton went over the evening. And those two manservants *hired* she said and so well scrubbed, as if boiled in their white gloves, and the soup and everything after it was stone cold. Oh, aunt Dalton wailed. She never could stand cold soup.

Because of his father Dalton Foster has always known how people stand during cocktails or pre-dinner drinks, one shoulder, one hip a little higher than the other, one knee bent slightly and one foot a little in front of the other. One hand high and cold, cold with the iced stem of the glass and the other hand in a pocket, if a man, and in the case of a woman, clutching the elbow of the wine-glass hand. This clear picture comes back to him as he approaches the remembered house. Sometimes, from the frozen semi-circle of well-bred conversation and delicate sippings, a knee could be seen to lean outwards to take secret support from the arm of a hideous chair or the corner of a sideboard.

Dalton, at the time, was old enough to know that his father was a disappointment to his mother. He knew too that his father's polished black shoes pinched and that he had once, on sitting down, exposed, without meaning to, the white untrodden soles and the polished insteps of these compulsory shoes. His mother, he remembers on that occasion, was wearing a dress which did not suit her and which was not improved by a double pearl choker. Without wanting to, he remembers her flushed cheeks and her unsuccessful attempts to attract his father's attention by repeatedly raising her eyebrows in his direction and looking at him with slightly parted lips. Dalton could have told his mother then, and before then, that his father was incapable of understanding the simplest messages of this sort.

As he walks, he thinks about the strange coincidence of being given, on discharge from the special part of the hospital, an address. It was called a contact address, he was told, of people who would be willing to receive him as a visitor if he needed somewhere to go. It turned out that the address was of a house where they, his father and mother, aunt Dalton and himself, had lived. The house apparently was still a house for an itinerant Consul and his family. He must, he remembers, have been about twelve when his father moved on. He remembers being quite young. Perhaps they had visited and lived in Australia more than once.

He was forced into further understanding of his place in society during his first visit there.

'I'm sorry, Betty, we can't come to bridge tonight,' he heard his hostess, her rich loud voice pouring into the telephone and spilling across the hall and into the library where he sat, in a deep chair, in the company of the children and their tutor.

'This is my discharged prisoner, *person* I should say, this is my discharged *person's* first visit here. He has just turned up this evening and I feel we should remain at home, just this time, you see, dear, because it is the *first time*. Alexis is not in yet but he will feel as I do ...'

'No dear,' the voice continued. It was an Australian voice enriched by fresh air and good food, a voice resulting from being reared on the spacious property of a wealthy pastoralist family overlaid, at some stage, by the effects of an expensive English boarding school for girls. 'No dear,' she said, 'I'm not in the least bit frightened, neither are the children, neither is Monsieur

Perdu. Yes, I realise he is not a bodyguard, but his presence, his elegant presence is a sort of protection even if it is not needed as such. But about our visitor – no, I am not certain about his age, I'd say it was indeterminate, I suppose it could be, yes, I suppose anything around forty plus. No, of course not eighty! Yes dear, brown, brown soft hair and a brown moustache and his brown eyes, I would say are heavy with the weariness of experience, revealing all he has been through. No, I'm not being poetical, dear. I am trying to tell you my impressions. He has a long, thin, sensitive nose, a musician's or a scholar's nose and ascetic lips, a thin mouth ... And, yes dear, a brown, rather shabby suit and a brown raincoat ... No dear, he's kept it on ... No dear, I'm not at all worried by the raincoat.' Her rich laugh pealed across the hall and into the library. 'Perhaps,' she laughed, 'he'll take it orf next time, on his next visit. He's coming again quite soon, he's not sleeping over this time though his bed's made up for him all in readiness. No, he doesn't just come once, he's allowed to come, sort of once a week, yes, that sort of thing. Yes dear, we knew beforehand his whole sad, unfortunate history. He has to be given the chance to make the *leap* from *that* to this ... No dear, he won't be spending the night when he sleeps over, in the lounge or the library, nor the spare room upstairs and no, no dear, not the music room, the *conservatory*, dear. I thought the conservatory – that way he has his own little bathroom. Yes, I agreed to his having a hot bath and one meal, dinner or breakfast. Yes dear, he can come once a week and the idea is that he leaves early, yes dear, *early*. It's just until he acclimatizes and gets used to the guest house where he's paid a month in advance for his room. The authorities, dear, don't want him to be entirely homeless, which he is of course. There are too many of *them* roaming about with nowhere to go. Yes dear, of course Ursula and Cornelius are safe. He isn't at all *dangerous*, dear, just terribly unfortunate. No, of course we're not going to be stabbed in our beds. And remember we do have our lovely young Monsieur Perdu, you remember the children's tutor? No, of course they're not children any more but we regard Monsieur Perdu as a sort of finishing school.' M. Perdu, preening, gave himself a little smile which he secretly hid in the lapels of his dressing gown.

'Mother's voice,' Ursula said quietly, 'can't be helped. She grew up yelling across paddocks and her sister also; they, when they were children, yelled at each other across miles of wheat stubble and sheep.'

Dalton Foster, sitting too much on the edge of a deep chintzy armchair was embarrassed. The smell of the glazed cotton brought back memories in rapid succession. He was not able to look up to meet Ursula's kind smile with a smile of his own.

'They all,' Cornelius leaned forward with his handsome boyish grin close to Dalton's face, 'Mother and her sister, our aunt, and all their friends *do* shout, it's simple, *they just do shout*.' He sat back with an amused and tolerant glance in the direction of the hall. 'They are more English than the English.'

'No, Betty dear,' the voice from the hall, persisting, was lower, as if out of regard for Dalton's presence, but still audible, the door not being closed properly. 'No, dear. We are not sure *exactly* why he has come out here to Australia. He was born here, apparently. His parents were English and, like us, dear, they were *on the move a great deal*. Such a bore in one way, and yet there are excitements in this kind of life ...' Another silence followed.

'Mother's sister talks as much as she does,' Cornelius said gently. 'Mother has to let auntie have her say. They have big, long telephone calls, all across the world sometimes. It's peaceful while auntie has her turn, so peaceful, isn't it,' he smiled in an indulgent way, leaning forward again towards Dalton as if to protect him from what might be said next.

'Well dear,' it was their mother's turn again, she lowered her voice as if something very private, a secret, had to be told. 'It seems that it was thought, I suppose by his doctor or medical officer, it was thought, dear, that he should have the chance to make a fresh start right away from the places which might bring back his trouble. Places are very important, dear, and especially *people*. He might, d'you see, dear, get in with the *wrong people* back there, but here he will simply have his childhood memories and these might well be very comforting. He does seem to be so completely alone, yes dear, I said alone –'

'Auntie's turn,' Cornelius announced in the silence which turned out to be brief.

'Yes, Betty dear, we shall put out the little folding bed for him,' the voice penetrated once more, 'it's all under control. We must do our bit, you know, so much poverty, suffering and loneliness in the world … No dear, no drugs, I was assured, no problems of *that* sort. The problem is, well, somewhat different, more intangible if you know what I mean. Alexis is very keen on rehabilitation. And you know his *continental* wishes, probably he's hoping for another instrument or a beautiful voice – whatever we have, it will make a sextet. Oops dear, sex!' In the cascade of laughter which followed, Cornelius, who looked about sixteen, put on a video cassette of some music. Dalton noticed his thin white wrists and the cord attached from his wrist to a small embroidery frame.

'Do you like music?' Ursula moved to another chair close to Dalton and asked him again, 'Do you like this music?' Dalton wanting to reply, saying that he did like music and, especially, this was very nice, could only nod and gulp once or twice in his shyness.

'Vivaldi,' Ursula said in a kind voice, as if to help him out of any awkwardness. '*The Four Seasons*,' she said. Next time he came, she told him, they would listen to the whole performance and watch the scenes. 'The pictures,' she explained, 'are really lovely. We'll listen to the whole thing. Would you like that?' She peered into his face.

Dalton nodded once more. Yes, thank you, he wanted to say, and yes he would like that very much. But no words came.

❧

There was a great deal more than could have been anticipated in this returning, this state of being cast back into what was called society. Dalton, as he walks, is used to the word society. It was a much-used word in the discussion groups.

❧

The husband, the father of Ursula and Cornelius, had come home just before Dalton left. They were all in the

44

hall when the father came in. He was a small handsome man; Dalton thought he would be nimble both in his body and his language. He spoke four fluently, often mixing words and phrases from all of them in one sentence. His chief interests, Dalton was told when they were all practically on the door mat, were art and music next, of course, to his family. The family made their own music, he told Dalton. They were a quartet. He hoped, he said, that Dalton would, at times, take part. They had, he said, already been told about his fine voice and superior musical knowledge.

Dalton, thinking over the brief visit, in retrospect, has to consider the surprises in that visit as calmly as possible. First there was the house itself, changed, of course, but still the same house even to the kind of curtains and the chair covers. Then there were the children. He had been told there were two children.

Sensible, the officer, Greyhead, in the prison hospital had said kindly to him. *Always say sensible to yourself.* Speaking as usual in single words or, at most, short phrases, Greyhead had been the one to offer, with reserve, advice.

The expected children, Ursula and Cornelius, were hardly children. They were tall, slender, handsome and privileged but had stopped being children. There was something hidden in the brother and the sister, an intimacy, a closeness which is enviable for those who do not possess it. It had its own difference. Dalton noticed at once the quick glances which had passed between them during the evening. And then there was the way in which both, when he was leaving, one after the other, had taken hold of his hand, almost snatching it, as if to linger in each other's caress on the hand of a stranger. These children, he thought, must be sixteen (Cornelius) and eighteen (Ursula), at least. Then there was the tutor. A very fortunate man, in Dalton's opinion, to be able to wear his well-cut dressing gown when partly, but fashionably, dressed. To add to this was the privilege of being acceptable while walking on the heels of his expensive leather slippers, smiling in a lazy but good-natured way, enjoying the prestige of his position in the household and, all the time, smoking his pipe with an aristocratic nonchalance.

It was clear that the children's mother, she of the rich loud voice, admired Monsieur Perdu very much and, in a fleshy way, she flirted with him. She wore a marocain dress. The crêpe material clung to her hips and was low in front so that her flesh, which was healthy and full, could be seen, flushed, in the deep scoops of the neckline. Dalton, embarrassed by her fluttering eyelids and the way in which her lips were drawn back over her teeth when she smiled, had looked down at the carpet. He was still studying the carpet when Alexis, the father, came home. The father, Dalton noticed with a shy glance, pranced. It was strange that the mother's smile recalled, for Dalton, a film star. He tried to think of the name. Katherine Hepburn, that was it. Not so strange, he told himself, while the father, prancing still, greeted his wife and children. Old films were shown on video every night in the special rehabilitation part of the hospital and he had been free to watch whenever he wanted. Briefly he realised he would miss the films and he was already missing the morning pots of tea they were allowed to make.

The Australian wife and mother, he thinks her name is Joan, seemed happy and contented to be back in her own country after spells, as she called them, in Paris, London and Japan.

'This endless travelling!' her laughter, pealing, sur-rounded her returned husband and the children. She explained what she called *the Rules* once more to Dalton who said he understood and that he was much obliged to them for their kindness.

'Much obliged,' he repeated the words to himself as he left the porch and made his way along the garden path to the gate.

Now he remembers the humble phrase, the 'much obliged', and realises it was an expression his father used.

In spite of the memory of his mother's and aunt Dalton's scorn, he supposes the words to be thoroughly suitable for the son of a Consul, a representative in trade.

As he walks Dalton understands that he is inadequate in more than mere money. He feels the invitation in the glances from Cornelius, his eyes almost closed, the long eyelashes dark on his white skin. Pursued, as he is by the glance, the quick movement of the head and the sight of the thin, white wrists of the boy, he pauses, listening for the shuffling of footsteps following him, disturbing the fallen leaves and twigs at the side of the road. There is always the thought that his fellow lodgers, the two on the same landing, across from his own door, are following him at some little distance. He has no explanation for this thought, only an uneasiness.

❧

Though he is now under Mrs Porter's roof he finds himself, with no real excuse, drawn towards the house where Cornelius and Ursula are sure to welcome him. He feels the wish to visit the house at a time of day when he should, if sleeping there, be leaving it. Perhaps, he thinks, the side door will be opened to him in a movement of hospitality and perhaps a kettle will be boiling ... He gives himself up momentarily, in an effort to walk on away from the house, to the subdued whisperings of his mother and his aunt, practically at the place where, in his previous thinking, he had left them.

'My dear, I declare I was so bored,' his mother whispered later that evening to his aunt. 'It was all I could do,' she said, 'to stay on my chair. And the food, my dear, *looked* handsome and was well served by those two well-laundered manservants but every mouthful was cold, not only the soup and *that*, don't you think, my dear, had a strange smell which I was quite unable to identify . . .'

The early morning suburban streets are unchanged except that the distances seem greater on some days.

The little girl is playing all alone in the park, solemnly going from one swing to the other. She goes up the rope ladder to the platform and down the slide. Sliding without a smile. She seems to be completely unmoved as she climbs the metal frame and hangs high by her arms. She wriggles through the hanging tyres and returns to the swinging bridge which she crosses three times in both directions, as in a ritual, seriously. Dalton Foster, watching her from the path, wants to walk over the grass to where she is. She does not smile, he is sure, because there is no one for her to smile at. His own face, he knows, is unsmiling and dull. There is no one to receive a smile from him either.

The little girl is not wearing enough clothes for the cold morning. She is ragged. For this park, in this suburb, an unusual raggedness. He corrects himself, the suburb is not as it once was. The child has bare feet and her uncut hair is uneven round her stalk of a neck. Her hair hangs over her eyes. Like a pony, Dalton thinks. A little horse all alone in the park. There is no mother waiting for her. He looks round quickly. No one is about. It would be nice to hold the little girl's hand and walk with her over the soft grass. Better still to have her close alongside him, at dusk perhaps, his arm about her thin little body, hugging her and both of them going home together. His lonely cold room at Mrs Porter's would be quite different with the child. Someone he could care for almost as one might care for a kitten. His raincoat is not very thick but would be warm enough. He would sleep on the floor and use his coat as a blanket. But he must be careful. Accusations come all too quickly to people who only mean well. Especially where children are concerned. He hopes she has no home.

He remembers the park well though this playground was not as it is now. The park seems smaller and the main road along one side much noisier. The long-leaved peppermint trees are the same and the freshness of the grass, the flame-tree flowers, the busy parrots and the magpies are all as they have been in his memory. There had been plenty of time to reflect, during the years, that one of the things about prison was that there was no grass and there were no flowers. Perhaps in going over, reliving certain experiences, it is possible to dismiss them.

%

He asked his mother and aunt Dalton what a Consul was.

'What is a Consul?' Just about here in this park he remembers his question.

'Why, Dalton, your father is a Consul.' His mother's mouth turned down at the corners as she raised her eyebrows at aunt Dalton. 'Why look, Dalton! There are your friends,' his mother went on. 'Go and play, Dalton. We shall be quite comfortable here on this bench.'

He remembers now that he thought then that women couldn't run. If they ran, Violette told him, all their insides would fall out, so they had to walk with tiny little steps keeping their legs close together. He remembers Violette and Leonie so vividly they could even now be coming towards him. They wore very short skirts and the waists of their dresses were wide and low. The hem of Violette's dress came exactly to that place where her legs would be joined together on her body. Both Violette and Leonie had fat legs which rubbed together with soft little noises when they walked. When they played, the little girls told him that his bucket of sand was the shopping and he was to bring it to their grass house. With their fat little hands the two girls patted and shaped the mown grass into little ridges. These are the walls, they explained, making little rooms. They decorated the grass house with little twigs and leaves and they set selected stones out as if spreading a table.

Come into the grass house, they said to Dalton, showing him which was the door. The grass house was theirs until some big boys, racing through the park, made a detour through the little soft walls. Dalton remembers now the black lace-up farm boots and the marks the boots left in the leaf mould and the soft sand. With the wild scattering of the sweet-smelling grass, Violette and Leonie, their cheeks flushing red, ran away, their fat legs flying out sideways.

'Our little wretch is very pale,' aunt Dalton remarked to his mother when he returned to their bench. As a child he was always pale, he knows this, because aunt Dalton was always saying so. Often she drew unwanted attention to the dark circles round his eyes, reminding him that he had not slept.

'What is a Consul exactly?' he remembers appealing to aunt Dalton, his mother having tossed away the whole subject with the little frown which always accompanied the subject of his father. His mother and aunt Dalton, on the bench where they had been sitting, were secretly hugging each other under their outdoor clothes.

'Let me see,' aunt Dalton said then, her eyes bright with her own mischief, 'Consuls have been in the family since Napoleon. You, you little darling, you little wretch, you look so like your mother, you will have to be a Consul one day. You must read your history book ...'

'Oh, Hermione!' his mother said then, interrupting. 'Heaven forbid!'

'Well, darling,' aunt Dalton said, 'you must save our little treasure. Put him to the piano and the violin and cherish his sweet voice. He must have singing lessons.'

❧

The ragged little girl is walking slowly, looking back sometimes, towards the station end of the park. As Dalton Foster turns to leave the playground to follow the child he remembers the fair which used to visit the park every year, and how, one year, he had been put on a horse for a ride. He had to stand on a high table to wait for his turn. A big girl led the horse and he had no idea, among the trees, where the horse and this girl would take him.

He sat up so straight, he heard aunt Dalton reminding his mother repeatedly. 'He sat up so *straight*, a bit pale perhaps but serious, my dear, he never smiled once. Mark my words,' aunt Dalton went on, 'our little wretch has had an *experience* and he isn't going to share it with us. We shall never know how he *felt* on the horse.'

❧

He supposes now that his mother and his aunt searched him for his experience. As he hurries after the little girl who is hopping now on one leg, one step forward and one back and every now and then peering through her shaggy hair in his direction, he is not sure that he really remembers being on the horse. What he remembers might only be what he has been told. Even Rose, he recalls, told him that he had had this horse ride. A horse walk, she called it. Something really sedate and safe and taken care of by an unknown girl. A gypsy perhaps. For several years it had been an exciting thought stored in his mind, kept there perhaps more by Rose.

'Rose,' his aunt Dalton said, 'we shall be out all day.'

'Rose will look after you,' his mother said, 'while your aunt Dalton and I are out all day.'

He made a strawberry jelly with Rose. He spilled the crystals all over the table top, thinking the jelly would be in firm squares, cubes really, shining dark-red cubes to be pulled apart, dark red like glass.

'Your mother won't see nor know,' Rose said, sweeping the pink sand into the bowl. 'What the eye don't see the heart don't grieve over. Now mind! the water's hot, boilin' hot, just don't you go scalding yourself.'

Dalton Foster remembers clearly the pleasure of stirring the hot jelly. He remembers the sharp sweet scent of it. Rose's scent.

'Oo's a lucky lucky little boy then.' Rose, when she had finished her baking, put him on her thigh to ride her like a horse. 'Lucky little boy to ride a cock horse.' She laughed and tickled him, riding her thigh faster and faster, lucky lucky little boy.

Later when the jelly was set he would not eat any of it and aunt Dalton, still in her hat and coat, kneeling by his chair begged him. 'Eat, pretty boy, you must eat,' as she begged him at times with scrambled eggs.

Disturbed and consoled by unexpected memories, Dalton Foster stands watching the little girl, the little playground pony. She has reached the main road and is about to pick her way through the traffic. He sets off quickly, determined now to keep her in sight. Probably she is making for the railway station. He sees the station as being a good place for him to catch up with her. He wants to follow the child. He wants to offer her things, for one thing, she does not know how to make a grass house. Just this once more he wants to promise. Already his thoughts are full of the things he will promise her. He wants to make these promises.

Mornings and evenings, it is as if Dalton Foster, whenever he walks away from Mrs Porter's place, is always on the way back to the house. As soon as he enters the house he feels closed in by the curtains and the chair covers. The glazed cotton, patterned with tiny English flowers, oak apples, leaves and acorns, envelops him. The smell of this clean cotton makes him want to leave at once and to go to some other place. This other place remains for ever undefined and undescribed. Because he has a room in Mrs Porter's establishment he has no real reason for returning to the house. All the same, as the days and weeks go by, he continues to walk there mornings and evenings. It does not take long to leave the derelict edges of the poorer side of the city, the railway yards and the back of the markets and then, by crossing a small park, he very soon reaches the quiet tree-lined streets of the suburbs and, of course, the house.

Mornings and evenings, whenever he walks either to or from the house, he watches and listens to the birds. Especially in the evenings, on the way there, with his heart full of hope he looks up to the tops of the sugar gums where the doves, in silent persistent divings, are driving other birds away from the roosting branches.

The green parrots are noisy with their screeching and complaining. They seem to outnumber the doves. As he pauses to watch them, he thinks of Tennyson's well-contented doves and the line from Wordsworth which had delighted him years earlier; *over its own sweet voice the stock dove broods.* Doves, always the symbols for peace, rounded and gentle and harmless, show a surprising difference in their qualities when attacking and driving off the parrots. It is clear that, as in human life, there is in nature more than one aspect presented for consideration.

In the early evening, at that time of the evening, when he is on his way towards the house, the trees are at their massive best because the sun is still reaching, with glowing light, into the higher branches and the topmost bunches of foliage. Unshed bark clings in rosy strips to the immense, grey tree trunks. Bark, half peeled and scattered, is warm. Discarded dry bark lies all round the trees for the whole length of the avenue. The whole way of the final approach to the house is made, in a sense, of all the passing seasons, one after the other, of broken, crumpled and twisted stripping of twigs and bark.

The squabbling of the birds at sunset disturbs Dalton Foster. He looks up to see the illumination of the birds and the leaves one more time. The brittle branches overhead, though cradle like, do not rock in the wind.

They remain rigid, their leaves, shivering and tremulous, catch with their trembling glittering surfaces the last light of the day. Because of looking upwards, in this way, it is possible for Dalton to think of the house with hope and a measure of restfulness.

Regret comes to him on his way back to Mrs Porter's place. As he walks back, every time, it seems as if he is returning to a temple devoted to regret. His unwanted thoughts are not always in the same sequence, they follow one after the other in a confusion.

As he walks he seems to walk in an emptiness. Hardly ever does he meet anyone during the walk. And, if he does pass someone else walking along the paths towards him, he looks aside and does not accept the intrusion of the spectatorial gaze.

Sometimes when he walks, he hears the light and sometimes shuffling sounds as if someone is following him. When he stands still for a moment there is no sound. When he resumes his walking there is often the unmistakable cracking of a twig or the rustling of dry bark at some little distance behind him. In daylight or in darkness he does not turn to look back along the way he has come.

Horsefly, they called him Horsefly. For as long as Dalton
Foster could remember his mother and his aunt Dalton
had called his father, Dalton Foster senior, Horsefly.
Behind his father's back they called him Horsefly. Dalton,
little Dalton, understood from an early age that Horsefly
was not a nice name. And, that it was a secret, like so
many other things, went without saying.

The spider in the bath that morning reminded Dalton
Foster of his mother, of the elegant way in which she
placed one foot, toe pointing, before the other when she
walked. Her heels, he remembers, hardly touched the
ground. When he considers his mother's feet he
understands that over the years he has noticed women's
feet and their ankles rather more than their faces or
their waists. The slender foot encased in fine leather,
and the well-bred way in which one shapely foot was
placed in front of the other, marked for him the kind
of woman and her country of origin. Because of his
father's work and position they moved frequently from
one place to another. When they were in England his
mother, fitting in, wore Heath hats and a burberry but

in spite of this, her feet remained, like the intonation in her speech, forever Viennese. She wept often.

'Why is mamma crying?' Dalton, knowing the answer, would call out during the night.

'She is homesick, that is all,' his father, creaking on alien floorboards, would explain, his voice hoarse with the attempted whisper, 'go to sleep.' Often aunt Dalton, his father's sister who always travelled with them, would pass with soft rustlings through Dalton's room to console his mother. They usually had, in hotels, a suite of adjoining rooms.

His mother and aunt Dalton would have laughed helplessly behind Mrs Porter's back had they had the misfortune to meet her and to foolishly take rooms in her establishment. Together they would have mocked her speech and given her a reticule, a shabby fox fur and dropped aitches. This was their way of dealing with the people and the places in which they were obliged to live.

Sometimes Dalton longs now for a share of gentle mockery and laughter putting someone else at a disadvantage, thus helping to ease the uneasiness and discomfort of trying to be at home in a strange place. It was watching the light delicate movements of the spider, unknowingly trapped on porcelain, which caused him to spend too much time having his long-awaited turn in the bathroom. His reverie was disturbed by a pounding on the door. The infected waiter, ashamed of his sickly appearance and his fellow lodger, the door man who seemed to be developing, to *his* shame, a bust, from the room across the passage wanted their turn.

∝

In analysing his position there are several factors to be taken into account, the main one being, for the moment, the electricity cut, due, Dalton supposes, to a strike or an accident somewhere. For some hours there has been complete darkness and the evening, as the time passes, seems colder than ever. There is a sense of silence and isolation and he is not able to decide whether to lie down or to remain sitting on his chair. Either on the chair or on the bed the darkness seems to strangle. A grey mistiness relieves the blackness if he glances up to his narrow strip of high window. But, after a few moments, this sense of relief passes and he is once more trying to breathe normally in the choking darkness. He longs for the sound of a train passing, the sound of the sad horn in the distance approaching the level crossing, and then the repeat of the horn, this sad little phrase of music, coming closer as it warns at the second level crossing. The long drawn-out rumbling of the wagons of the wheat train as it fills the night would be both a reminder and a reassurance that there were serene places where people were engaged in fearless investigations of things like sea weed, water-flow, underground minerals, the growing of crops and the education of children. The song of the brave horn reminded that there was a world beyond the houseful of discarded men and women. Earlier he had groped his way to the door to open it with the hope that a candle and matches might be on the way. The usual sounds of the subdued living in the house seemed then to have disappeared completely as if something sinister was about to take place. He had shut his door quickly with the feeling that instead of the passage immediately outside there was an unexpected and unexplained enlargement of the stairwell, an abyss into which he would fall. Feeling his way back to the chair he had experienced a momentary sense of safety. A sense, he realises almost at once, bordering on hallucination.

He wonders whether Miss Mallow is suffering quietly in the room below. Because of the damp, her room will be even colder than his. Like himself, Miss Mallow must sometimes consider her reason for being alive and for having come to lodge in Mrs Porter's Guest House. He remembers reading somewhere that Chekhov said that all people should consider leaving something behind, perhaps a school or a well. What could Miss Mallow leave, except a thin trail of unsatisfactory music lessons? Miss Mallow, with vague hopes of leaving Mrs Porter's, has shown him her useless reference three times now.

'In case you should hear of something,' she said on every occasion, unfolding the thin sheet of paper and revealing the now unacceptable compliments in the tremulous handwriting of someone very old.

This is the first time, he has to understand, the first time in his life that he has lived alone. Strictly speaking he is not living alone. The breakfast table, in its bleakness, seats between eight and ten people for a very short time every day. Every breakfast is accompanied by the wish that there was some reason, apart from the impatience of Mrs Porter on behalf of her maid, for hurrying away. He wishes often, and particularly now in the dark, for life as it once was. He wishes he could sit at a table, preferably one with a plush cloth in a warm room, reading and writing – wasn't it Johnson who said: *The greatest part of a writer's time is spent in reading in order to write: a man will turn over half a library to make one book* – knowing that at suitable intervals he would be called to meals, pleasant with the amusing conversation of his mother and his aunt, their mood lightened in the absence of his father. He could, he knows, have been distinguished in scholarly thinking and writing. His papers are somewhere in the never-unpacked part of his luggage. As soon as he can, when there is a light, he will, he thinks, take out the work and read all through it, and then start a massive rewriting, something along the lines of the development of the musician's philosophy, not a poem but a long prose work with emphasis on the passionate wish for truth with elements of emotion and feeling in exact proportions to the whole. He will endeavour to have a style for the writing, using the power of restraint, hesitant at times, even to being somewhat withdrawn ...

This continuation of darkness and silence seems to herald a disaster, something big, a national disaster. Perhaps something has already happened and he, Dalton Foster, is the only human being alive, by some strange fluke, in a destroyed universe. He longs to call out for a light. He is unable to stop shivering. He hopes for a gleam of light to show under the door as he used to see it, when he was a very small child, before the servants had all gone to bed. If the single electric light should come on he will start at once to write. It is his intention now to sit in this room and to write everything that has happened to him since those days when he spent hours half sitting and half lying at the edge of the green corn. Wheat to be exact, sturdy stemmed, packed close with heavy ears, in a small field which met, unfenced, the sweet-smelling trampled grass of the river bank where thick-set cows, the colour of cream, waited patiently to be herded for milking. Those days from which he must start writing were in summer in England. It should not be difficult, in time, to include everything from before his illness. Before what, after his prison sentence, was declared an illness, requiring prolonged and voluntarily repeated treatment. In his writing he will be able to dwell with freedom in the forbidden memories. Often, like now in the darkness, it has seemed that he is so near to that place he has only to stretch out a hand and feel again the smooth stonework, its silkiness more like folds of drapery than stone. The sense of a previously unknown happiness which accompanied his first years in the place of study and easy, enlightening conversations and, perhaps more importantly, friendship, returns unbidden. And there, half hidden in the golden haze of sunlight streaming through stained glass, would be the returning vision of the boy's golden curls touched here and there with red and green and purple reflections. And, in the warm light of the peaceful solitude, the child's small knees, in their perfection, would glow. The long sleepy summer afternoon, the images of cathedral, meadow, cows and cornfield dissolve all too quickly in a shedding of tears as Dalton weeps once more alone in his lightless room. It was the sweetest intention and the interruption of the intention, and then the enforced reliving of these in public during the repeated sessions of cure, rehabilitation it was called, which were, and are still in thought, unbearable. The intervening years have not softened or erased anything.

⁂

When investigations into corruption are carried out they are often examined internally by the organisation concerned. Dalton's habit of consolation lies in a pattern of repetitious thought. For example, he considers the ways in which a government department or a financial institution will undergo an expensive lengthy formality, skimming across the facts with one meaningless cliché after another so that the outcome will appear to be satisfactory. The real blame is never exposed and victims remain unrecompensed and the evil, like a bad smell, persists. A smell comparable with that which is sometimes present in summer from an abattoir which is never thoroughly cleaned. Rotting and putrid offal is left clinging to cogs which should be clean and shining. Something is left to go on rotting in certain investigations. But when an ordinary man is accused and a search is made upon his life it is as if ferrets are set upon him and his whole private existence is turned inside out. Nothing is skimmed over, explained or denied, and he has to face whatever punishment and whatever painful cure is ordered.

As he crouches on his single chair he is forced to consider his all too recent disturbing contemplations. He should never, earlier this evening, have followed the little girl. She, in her ragged clothes and her small innocence, seemed to want him to follow her.

He is haunted now, partly by his own imagination, by the glimpse of the threatening behaviour of the group of people to whom, in an unspoken way, the little girl seemed to belong. His action in following her could cause him harm and alienate him once more and for ever. At the same time he is not certain that the child belonged to those rough-looking people who seemed to form the edge of a small and nebulous crowd into which she disappeared.

'Sometimes,' the judge said, 'people alienate themselves from their environment. This is what you have done.' The doctor, when he was talking to Dalton, simply told him that he had, for the time being, cut himself off from home. It was only a temporary thing, he said, adding that it was a part of his work to get him back there.

Sitting in the cold room waiting for the light to come

on once more, it is as if an unbridgeable distance of space and years separate him from what the doctor spoke about as home.

The doctor, at the time, spoke about a sort of half-way existence, a large and careful step to be taken from the life in the institution to the life in society and all its changes. It was not possible, the doctor made it clear, to have life again as it once was. This, he said, was a true fact about everyone's life and not simply in the circumstances which were called rehabilitation.

Being alone in darkness and silence seems to increase the sense of airlessness. Accustomed to circumventing discomfort and uneasiness, Dalton Foster recalls other wise advice. The rehabilitation officer, prematurely grey and corpulent, never said a great deal. He would fix his ice-blue gaze on the face of the person he was addressing and deliver his remark in the shortest way possible. *Be sensible*, was one phrase, *think ahead* was another, and *on guard* was a third. The shortness of speech was prolonged, during delivery, by a penetrating stare. In contrast his face was genial with a flush of red on the nose and on both cheeks.

Dalton, at the time, needing to bring the consolation of the once pleasant and familiar, likened him, in silence, to the ancient poet, Horace, whose shape had, at one time, been compared, by a friend, to that of a thick little book.

> *Grown grey before my Time,*
> *I hate the cold and seek the warmth ...*

Greyhead's longest phrase being *cold enough to freeze the balls off a brass monkey*, often shortened to *freeze the balls*, caused Dalton, even in those circumstances, uncongenial to poetry and to people who loved books, to hold, still in the silence of his mind, the rhythm as if his speaking self would, all at once, recite the ode, at the same time, imagining Mr Greyhead having a private life embedded in the innocent simplicity Horace himself was said to have chosen.

> *Olives and Mallows deck my Board,*
> *The wholesome vegetable kind;*
> *O let me thus alone be flor'd,*
> *With Health of Body, Health of Mind.*

Horace, choosing simplicity, composed verses like a gentleman, rather than as a poet by profession. Dalton, meeting Greyhead's stare and his brief words of advice, longed to have the rhythm in his own mind taken up and passed back to him. He wished then for study and for literature and the grace which accompanies discussion. He thought about books and how necessary they were to life. In the absence of all these he held on to them in his thoughts, knowing that he was not, in any way, *changed for the better* (another of Greyhead's phrases), but understanding that very serious attempts were being made on his behalf.

Greyhead, walking with him to the outer doors, carrying the folded raincoat over his arm, passed it across in a manner which was almost ceremonial saying, as if out of habit, in his husky voice: *Be sensible,* adding as if for good measure, that there *was no call for him, ever in the future, to touch his toes for anyone.*

'The trouble with my kind of work, you know, being a representative in trade,' Dalton's father said to him on one of the rare occasions when they were alone together, 'is that we're on the move the whole time. Like the gypsies,' he said, giving a little laugh of apology. 'Except,' he went on, 'we don't have horses and I don't make clothes pegs and mend kettles.' They were on bicycles that day. Dalton's was a fairy cycle with blown-up tyres and he had a small black rabbit in a paper carrier bag on the handlebars. His father's bicycle, built by himself from parts selected from stalls and shops, was very high. To watch his father mount his cycle, the way in which he scooted along and then threw one leg up and over, was both miraculous and laughable to Dalton. Laughable because it was the custom of his mother and his aunt, his father's sister, to laugh at him. His father spoke with a north of England accent with the short 'a' sound in words like bath and path. When Dalton, after being with his father, adopted this short 'a', his mother or aunt Dalton, or both of them together, corrected him, pouncing on the offending words.

'Barth, Dalton, dear boy, and Parth,' bringing the vowel sounds down through their noses, as they declared, people who had been to university in Oxford did.

'The short "a",' his mother sighed, 'is such a stigma.' Sometimes she corrected Dalton's father who, on such occasions, looked at her with a sort of baffled surprise.

'I can't think,' Dalton's mother would say later to aunt Dalton, 'how I married that vowel,' and both would laugh, aunt Dalton reminding, with generous caresses, that in the event of Dalton's mother not marrying Dalton T. (T for Trade) they might never have really known each other.

On the day Dalton remembers now, his father was restless in the absence of Dalton's mother and aunt. He seemed white faced and excited. He stuffed a few things in a small rucksack, which perched like an irregular hump on his back. He put on cycle clips and a green eye shade and told Dalton to hurry with his breakfast.

'We're off into the country,' he said and Dalton had to remind him about the rabbit.

'We'll take her too,' his father said.

It was to let the rabbit out that they stopped. Leaning their bicycles in the ditch they crawled through the hedge and the rabbit hopped and paused uncertainly at the edge of a crop which Dalton's father thought might be barley.

'A barley field,' he said, lying back in the sun gazing contentedly through his green shade. Bent double, Dalton followed the slow hops of the rabbit, bringing her back to his father's side whenever she seemed to be straying a little too far.

'When I was a boy I kept rabbits,' Dalton's father said suddenly. 'We ett 'em,' he said. 'There's nothing as nice as rabbit stew, a good rabbit stew.' As the rabbit seemed content not to wander, Dalton's father told Dalton to rest his legs as they had quite a bit to pedal before they would reach the guest house.

'We're right on the edge of the Wyre forest,' Dalton's father said. 'Not my homeland exactly but it'll do.' He was hoping, he said, as he had hoped before, to find Dalton's mother and his aunt. He pronounced aunt as ant. 'Your anty,' he said, 'she was always up to mischief. She were a lass and half when she were your age.' He laughed his small shy laugh. 'I used to visit your Grannie years ago in hospital,' Dalton's father went on. 'I used to sit by her, "Mother," I'd say, "You're not saying much." "Oh," she'd say, "I've said all I've got to say." She was past ninety then.'

In the ward across the passage, Dalton's father explained that day on the edge of the barley, there was an old man of about ninety-seven. 'Every day,' Dalton's father said, 'a very talkative woman used to visit this old man. She wouldn't stop talking. Even when he was asleep she'd show him pictures in magazines and books. She'd read aloud to him and tell him things. She'd rouse him up and make him walk down the passage on his walking frame and he'd be hardly able to stand up. She brought in the newspapers and insisted on telling him all that was in them. I got irritated with her, though of course I never said so.' Dalton's father paused and shook his head as if in disbelief. Dalton felt embarrassed, he had never heard his father say so much to him at one time. After a few moments his father began to talk again. Dalton, with a knowledge beyond his years, feared a confession.

'And then,' his father said, 'all at once I had to see that she was missing him. Though he was alive, he was not how he used to be. The companion for life she'd had once upon a time was no longer there. She kept bringing in new clothes for him, things he'd never have a reason to wear. I saw,' his father went on, even though Dalton sat coldly narrowing his eyes towards the horizon. 'I saw,' his father repeated, 'that she was trying to bring back his tired memory and his withered body for him to be there for her as he once had been. She was not bereaved, do you see Dalton, by death, but by his old age. His old age had taken away her heartland.'

As Dalton reached out to his rabbit he saw, with a tiny side-long look, that tears were slowly overflowing from his father's eyes. He was weeping at the edge of the barley, it seemed, for someone he did not even know.

Dalton had learned early from his mother and his aunt to despise his father, to think of him (if he thought of him at all) as Horsefly. Though his father's position was an important one carrying responsibility, in their eyes it was despicable.

'A Consul, yes,' his mother would say, 'but oh! why *Trade* of all things!' Her wailings were heard frequently from behind closed doors in either the rented houses or the less fashionable hotels where they were often obliged to stay.

In the face of his father's grief, Dalton did not know what to say or do. Without a word he picked up the rabbit and, putting her in the paper carrier, he walked all along the edge of the barley to the gate. He climbed the gate and walked back along to his bicycle. Slowly he raised his bicycle from the shallow ditch and, hanging the paper bag on his handlebars, he began to pedal off along the road, riding close into the fringes of the tall grass and the cow parsley of summer. He could not help knowing that at the guest house his mother and his aunt, when they came in laughing and intimate like lovers, fresh and happy from walking through the leafy little lanes, would stand open mouthed with dismay at finding the Horsefly and little Dalton, dishevelled, at the reception desk in the hall.

And later at the evening meal his father who, in different circumstances, from the railway-station platforms to steamship wharves and landings, had done all this chasing many times before, made the clumsy remark, half in jest, that the great saddle of beef was, in fact, fit only to be a saddle. Without looking at his wife and sister, his conversation was intended for them, though he appeared always as if addressing the Misses Galbraith whose guest house it was and who, in turn, did not find the reference to their beef in the least amusing.

Dalton sensing, as usual, the need for a diversion drew the rabbit from under his jumper and let her hop between the vegetable dishes and the gravy boat on the polished table. As the frowns deepened in the glances between the Misses Galbraith, Dalton's mother and aunt, unable to control their mirth, shrieked with laughter and simulated reprimand while, at the same time, showing their delight at Dalton's success in humiliating his father.

The game of catching up with his father is a part of the ritual of falling asleep. Dalton walks fast, following his father who is a long way ahead of him on a road which shines wet as after a rainstorm. He walks faster as if he could overtake his father. The light of the evening is grey and a mist hovers on both sides of the road. Even when the mist swirls across the road, Dalton can still make out the figure of his father. He feels that if he could be walking alongside, instead of forever following, he would be able, at last, to tell his father the words he could never say. His father's hair, in this vision, is brown as on the day at the edge of the barley — and not white all round his head as it was later. And, in this game of catching up, there is no place for any name, for example, Horsefly. Simply the man ahead, always beyond his reach, is his father.

Headline: GRANDFATHER ABUSES TWINS

Mrs Porter: All of thirty years ago. I arsk you. Dragging something up with them married with kiddies.

They're after his money you can bet your life they are. The *Both* of them.

I'll bet a forchoon they've put their heads together and made it all up. And him living in a small place too – think of all the talk …

MENU – For the eligible only

Prawns in garlic rosemary
    and white wine (frozen TV dinners)
Prawns in Haitch P Sauce (as above)
Mashed potato
Table decoration: Lettuce
Dessert Caramel cream custard (individual serves)
    Tea
    Bingo

Mrs Porter: In your tea leaves EV
I see the signs. Mr Right is close by
Go to the atrium
    (supermarket)
12 noon and sit there
Mr Right could be passing

Miss Vales: I haven't seen him yet and I've been up and down the stairs all night nearly.

Mrs Porter: Go to the supermarket EV
If you never never go
You'll never never know.

Don't you cry EV
Here, have a prawn.

Dalton, guessing that Miss Vales is blessed with the same greedy curiosity as Mrs Porter, turns back from his usual walk, intending to return earlier than usual. The collar of his raincoat, though turned up, is useless against the rain. He has left his note books out and open on the little table in his room. Uneasy because of this, he is striding rather than just walking. He imagines Miss Vales peering at his written pages. He thinks of her heels tapping across the landing, across the strip of thin carpet and across the linoleum in his room. He has come to recognise the impatience in these tapping heels. The words he has written seem unwise and foolish when exposed to Miss Vales. He wishes he had put the note books away as usual.

Human life is everywhere a state in which much is to be endured and little to be enjoyed.

He remembers the double row of ornamental question marks he has arranged round this quotation. He wonders what she could possibly think about the question marks and his careful handwriting. He knows, too, that this stupid thought is purely to prevent an anxious one, that of her seeing and actually understanding what he has written, thus making him and the words a subject for future gossip.

He enters the house as quietly as possible. Somewhere in the house Mrs Disley is singing her songs of praise while dislodging the various infestations inhabiting the old building. He takes off his wet raincoat and hangs it on one of the hooks in the hall. He pauses, listening, not sure if Miss Vales is really in his room peering at his private words or whether this is simply a thought, something imagined. Miss Vales might think his handwriting is strange and unreadable. She might well not understand the passage he has written.

Accusation (she could be reading), *one half of the family accuses the other half. The ebullient young doctor made this statement. He said that people, afraid of sexuality or what they considered to be deviant sexuality, needing to blame, accused someone. Not openly, but with glancings and mutterings. Sometimes they stroked their own thighs while describing their accusations or they patted themselves with complacent gestures, saying that they themselves were perfectly normal in the areas they were patting. All the doctors were very young. Young and very keen, persisting in giving us what Ibsen called the lie, the life lie — that is, a title which was not real but which made us all into something; the poet, the philosopher, the teacher, the carpenter, the gymnast and the chef and avoiding such labels as the rapist, the victim, the thief and the scavenger. We all had these masks to replace the ones which were removed, dissolved in the slowly uttered truths during our first meetings after admission . . .*

He feels certain that Miss Vales is up there in his room, licking her thumb and forefinger as she flicks the pages over. He is breathing in, unwillingly, her perfume which, in the hall and on the stairs, is more powerful than Mrs Disley's disinfectant. She is probably bending over his table still and reading quickly. She would be a quick reader. She has that quick way about her, that nimble way that people who have had to look after themselves, all their lives, do have. He has noticed this. These people they never missed an opportunity. Others, like himself, were slow and diffident, almost leisurely, always postponing, putting off whatever had to be done. They did not make the most of the passing moment and the chance. They missed the last train or bus, and they missed the last slice of bread and the last apple, and they never saw the one and only friendly look or greeting. They had no faith in themselves or in anyone else and so were too slow or too late ...

Still standing in the hall, terrified of a meeting, a confrontation on the threshold of what should be his own private room, Dalton listens, trying to discover if someone is upstairs in his room. He hears suddenly a small crescendo, but hushed, of voices from the other side of the baize door at the far end of the passage. Miss Vales is telling, in rising sounds, that she remembers a serial on TV all about young doctors. She is saying that she's managed to have a good read and it's all about young doctors and very exciting just like the television. She has managed to read everything upstairs and 'it's like – real, like exciting'.

Moving down the hall, his heart thumping, Dalton hears Mrs Porter telling Miss Vales that she had better get right back up them stairs. 'You'd better pop right back, EV, I mean he never speaks. You can't get married, EV,' Mrs Porter is insisting, 'to a man you don't know. You need not know him all that much. Men, they're all reelly the same, but you must have a bit of an *idea*.' The voice, as in a dream, fades and then comes back, as if closer.

'Breakfasts aren't any use, EV. It's always him having been and gone. It's a case of popping back up to have another quick peek and then lock his door and come away down. Here, take the keys.'

'It's like, like on TV,' Miss Vales says. 'Ooh, it's ever so exciting. Real life in TV, young doctors ...'

'Go on then, look sharp,' Mrs Porter seems very close, 'with all this rain, you can't be sure he'll stay out there. He could be back any minute. Orf you go ...'

Dalton has noticed the horse-shoe-shaped hoop hung with mysterious keys. It is not difficult to imagine, exactly, Mrs Porter handing over the master key. Quickly putting on his wet raincoat, he wrenches open the front door and, stepping into the rivulets of water, he pulls the door closed as quietly as possible. He is not certain if he really heard them talking on the other side of the door. He could have imagined the whole conversation. A returning sense of homelessness envelops him as he considers a walk under the dripping trees in the park, or a visit to the house at such an unusual time. His unexpected arrival at the house might be met with embarrassment and confusion. In any case he is aware that his present, dejected and unattractive appearance would make the deep scars in his personality and his worthlessness more apparent.

At the end of the street he pauses again uncertain, and without confidence and direction. At all costs he must not surprise Miss Vales during her investigation.

The park is deserted, deeply green and tranquil in the rain mist. Dalton knows that a tranquil place cannot offer tranquillity when it is most needed. He walks without purpose for a few minutes and then turns back the way he has come, recalling all too easily the eager desperation embodied in Miss Vales, in her speech, her gestures and, in particular, in her eyes. The careful applications from little jars and bottles can never take away or hide the dark circles, the weary gaze of endless hope and repeated disappointment.

The idea that he is being considered by the two

women for a marriage with one of them is ludicrous, so much so that he thinks he is hallucinating, imagining frightening circumstances which might happen, therefore causing the miseries of the present existence to be unimportant in the threat of this greater ordeal. He knows himself enough to fear his own reaction, should an act of chivalry be demanded.

Dalton, knowing that he has nothing, except the need for shelter, in common with Mrs Porter's other guests, feels he must avoid their questions and their opinions. He feels, at times, that he should apologise and explain to someone about himself. If he did speak, he knows he would tell too much. Attempts at self-justification are often not understood, so he does not try to explain. Except for the smallest sound of greeting, he does not offer himself in speech.

A boarding house, especially a cheap one, has little privacy. Mrs Porter, without the merest hint of affection or kindness, achieves an unpleasant vulgar familiarity. Dalton recalls with longing, hotels with professional and friendly staff. Especially he remembers well-lit, well-polished reception desks attended by neatly uniformed officials who received and handed over keys. Every movement was accompanied with a little flourish and a smile of unquestioning good service and welcome.

Alone in his room he quickly puts the note books away. Glancing up at the small windows he feels shut in by the rain clouds which seem to be resting on the panes. Unable to be warm and to think clearly he weeps, without sound, drawing breath painfully and, at the same time, deeply ashamed. A different sort of man would thump on the baize door and enter the kitchen. He would joke with, and tease, the dancers, he would wink knowingly at Mrs Disley and at Miss Vales. He would be given a hot drink, perhaps some soup. He would be warm and dry in no time. But he is not this different sort of man.

The precarious moment passes as Dalton, warmed with the effort of grief, finds the consolation he needs in stored words and phrases and in images also hoarded. A return in thought to a particular kind of innocence repairs the fractures and bruises in the heart and the mind. He thinks, with a small tender smile, of the little girl and the kind of home coming they could have every day together. He thinks of the ways in which he could care for her and look after her. The small child, perhaps on the edge of unthinkable fear herself, would find serenity in his eyes and in the sound of his voice when he was singing her to sleep.

Such inexpressible joy collides briefly with the reality of the impossible. His happy state of mind moves once more towards the anxious and he tries to concentrate on the way in which a poem or a picture, an art form, can take suffering and, from it, can create something new, separate and full of beauty. Art atones, makes an atonement, and brings, in a healing way, sorrow back once more to joy.

Next time he will watch and follow the little girl closely, much more closely.

The thin legs of the child dance ahead of him as he waits to cross the road. She, not waiting for the lights to change, hops back and forth and runs between the cars and buses. Dalton, not wishing to, remembers the way in which his father, at one time when they were living in Paris, accompanied him to school. It was only a short walk but he was still young enough, his father thought then, to be guided wordlessly across the main road. The idea was that the father followed the son at a respectful distance, the son pausing at the crossing for the father to catch up. They then, in silence and in step, crossed together between the impatient lines of traffic and parted, still wordless, on the other side of the street. The boy, at once turning to the iron gate of the *lycée* and the father, in the opposite direction, to his *bureau*.

One morning there was a longer pause and the two of them stood, a point of interest to a passing *gendarme* and his fellow officer.

'This man is following you?' The officers turned and addressed Dalton. 'This man? He is following you? This man? He is troubling you? This man he annoys you? Yes? This man!'

Dalton already conscious, by this time, of his finely made features and his increasing height simply glanced at the officers and shrugged his shoulders. He did not even look at his father but crossed the street alone, leaving his father, whose elementary French, he knew, would not be up to dealing with the crude cautioning which was already catching the attention of other people, causing them to turn their heads and raise their eyebrows as they passed.

And now, as Dalton crosses the road, he finds he has lost sight of the little girl. Hurrying, breathing hard, bending forward, impatient with himself, having only one wish, that of catching up with her, he continues uphill to the station.

His father, he understands, would have consoled himself immediately with his latest products to be described for a trade meeting. It is only now, years later, that Dalton begins to understand his father's love and how it sustained him. In this instance it was his love for the bristle, the pure bristle of good brushes and the gold-edged labels accompanying the fine-quality hair brushes for ladies and for gentlemen. The little labels, attached with gold threads, and which bore the marvellous words, 'Anthrax Impossible', in gold Roman had so excited his father, Dalton had been obliged to turn away when shown some samples. There were the household brushes too, the one for high dusting and the one for sweeping and another for polishing and yet another for verandahs and for garden houses and paths. There were brushes for shoes, for boots, for stoves, for dogs and horses and more – for clothes, for fur, for velour, for suede, for silk and there was a soft little brush for a baby's head. Everyone, Dalton's father said when he held the soft little brush, everyone has had this little brush, at one time, smoothing their baby hair. All this is what it means to be in Trade; Dalton's father would have comforted his son the whole day at school, during the geometry class and the chemistry class and during mathematics when the little street corner scene persisted with its intrusive pain, the secret pain in the heart which cannot be allowed to pass the lips, throughout the morning and, without remedy, into the afternoon.

All this is forever close and vivid, returning at times as if there are still the whisperings between his mother and aunt Dalton nearby.

'Horsefly?'

'Horsefly, perhaps it should be Horsebrush, my dear.'

'No, it's Horsefly. Of course it's Horsefly.'

'Yes, of course.'

More out of breath than ever, he hears with annoyance, the two trains from opposite directions pull in alongside the all-too-distant platforms. He is aware that they have stopped and are now starting off once more passing each other, one in either direction, slowly at first and then gathering speed. He supposes that she must be in one of the trains, each one now disappearing on its own great curve of railway line away from the station.

He pauses, studying the timber of the footbridge as if seeing its impersonal sturdiness for the first time. He looks down along the platforms, deserted and as if unused when cleared of passengers. One of the circular flower beds, he notices with a sudden attention to detail, for him an instant remedy in the face of disappointment, is a floral clock. The enormous hands, weighed down with moss and little tufts of flowers, show the time to be about half-past nine. The child could be going anywhere. He has no idea where she came from and why she was playing alone in the deserted park.

He walks back the way he has come, down across the main road and into the park where he walks lightly across the green slopes making his way, yet again to the house. Perhaps someone will be playing the piano there, practising. The violin too, perhaps both, brother and sister, will be practising and he will be able to listen. Next time he will follow the little girl at once. He will not be slow next time. He will be in the park earlier. He thinks of the sweets he will have for her. He wants to give her something pretty as well, perhaps some hair ribbons or some lace.

Greek is like lace, he remembers the quotation from something said by Johnson and he tries to recall the rest of it, something like: *a man will get as much of it as he can.*

Now on the way to the house he can dwell on the idea of being safe in the household. He can dismiss the thought that he is being followed and watched in a sinister way as he knows people who are put back into the outside world often are watched and *set up* and dragged down. He has to remember, as well, that he should not visit the house more often than, perhaps, one night and one afternoon a week, and certainly not first thing in the morning.

It is the idea of the child which suggests possibilities. Her presence suggests the provision of warmth and childish noise and childish meals. Her presence suggests seclusion while she sleeps, and things like the comfortable airing of damp clothes and the brushing of her soft hair when she wakes up. He tries to think of something made of lace, the kind of things Ursula would wear, though she is very much older. He recalls something else about lace. Someone is supposed to have said, 'Babies eat their own lace.' He smiles, the little girl is too grown up to do anything like that. The little girl is no longer a baby. She is far too knowing, even he can see that.

As he walks, he does not think of the way back. Instead he considers the likeness between Greek and lace. He supposes that both are non-essentials in the face of Latin which, as he was taught, is essential.

In the same way that a certain route is followed back and forth along the same road, it is possible that certain thoughts accompany one direction and their order is reversed when travelling, walking that is, in the other direction. During these journeys there are, on different days, distractions. One of these is contained in the sturdy bent legs as athletes on the college playing field, in training, run backwards *en masse*, all of them together running in reverse; a curious stampede.

Mornings and evenings he is always on the way there or on the way back. It is on the return walk, especially at dusk, that the wind rushes up the avenue and the now sombre trees, massive and arching overhead, meet in a sinister darkness. His own light footsteps crackle with surprising noise on the dry sticks and bark. Dwarfed by the size of the trees he is insignificant and close to the earth. Every small sound of every reluctant footfall is a reminder of the inevitable return to Mrs Porter's establishment. With every step her house inches itself towards him. The green parrots and the doves, hidden in the blackness above, make no sound.

The road slopes downhill towards the river which offers a small triangle of light, water being the last thing to get dark. He first noticed this quality about water when he was a student. A gypsy snatch at twilight, someone said then, as they sat watching the pale warm evening of the English summer turn to night. Only the smooth curve of river water still gleamed with that light which persists long after grass and sky have melted into an all consuming darkness. His thoughts return all too often to those times, to the unwanted recognition of love between other people. This love belonged to the two friends who were studying for the tripos, as he was, at Cambridge. Exclusive and possessive, these two, in a heightened happiness, were contained in completeness in each other until one of them, turning away, came to Dalton's rooms. Dalton, protesting his surprise and lack of understanding, received with the all encompassing power of desire, his experienced and ardent lover.

His lack of understanding, he knew at the time and later, was merely an innocent pretence, an armour shielding reticence.

He thinks now that, if he remembers correctly, it was Socrates who was supposed to have said that the lover is nearer the divine than the beloved; for the god is in the one but not in the other; and perhaps this is the most tender of all thoughts and possibly is the source of all the treachery and the secret happiness the lover knows. Feeling, at the time, that he was the beloved he questioned this but only carelessly and, in turn, became the lover and felt he was the supreme owner, his mind bowing down in homage before beauty. He learned it was possible to cross the boundaries of the mind and the heart. He found a serene joy in the knowledge that thought can enter completely into feeling and feeling can enter completely into thought. This then was the happiness which brings peace of mind in a single heart beat. He found he was ready to leap from one literary discovery to another. He wanted to discuss and explain that the alleged typically Renaissance confusion of the Classical and the Biblical was really an inheritance from the Middle Ages which had no historical sense. It seemed clear to him that Chaucer had taken both Virgil and

Isaiah as a part of his intellectual background, dividing them with no apparent division. He entered discussion with a pure eagerness for the ultimate in understanding, and his argument was not intended to cause his literary opponents to lose face. And so, with an increasingly heightened happiness and energy, he received his mother and aunt Dalton, both in flowered chiffon and broad-brimmed hats, for afternoon tea in his rooms, quite unaware as he chose and paid for a box of cakes, of the events which were building up to burst upon him and to alter his life.

It is as if he has only to step off the road to one side and he would, at once, leave the brittle spread of leaves and little sticks fallen, to fill the shadows of the sugar gums and be walking with light steps across the water meadows, familiar still in his memory, inhaling the sweet breath of the herded cows, and on to that single pathway where one man must walk behind the other on the narrow strip between the closely packed, short-stemmed, ripening corn. Quickening his step, as he did then, he easily remembers that it had seemed to him that there was, in this new life in the university, a sense of freedom. It was the same feeling of freedom which could have been experienced by a boy removed from the hard life of his rural background in Ancient Greece and, unexpectedly, excelling in the strength and beauty and grace within the palaestra. He easily remembers his own high-pitched laughing and shouting, his own surprise at the incoherent language of excited happiness in the complete trust which accompanies the sudden deep friendship and the hoped for secret pleasures. These were all the sweeter because he had not expected them. And beauty too, unexpected, was in its purity, the new possession of the aesthete he secretly hoped to be. He began to feel, then, his own excellence.

And then, at the height of it, there was the suicide, *their* double death, *their* suicide, their death together.

✧

A roof-top suicide. A double-death pact. Unwanted headlines later made the announcement. It was something between the two of *them* from which he was, in the end, excluded. Something discovered early on the Sunday morning by the head gardener of one of the colleges. The head gardener simply inspecting, in readiness for visitors, a famous herbaceous border, had suddenly become, with him, an unwilling participator in grief. The news spread long before the arrival of the lunchtime cold sideboards. The supposition and discussion continuing in spite of everyone knowing.

In a few seconds now it is as if he has continued to step away from the crackling twigs and bark, noisy underfoot, and is walking in a nervous hurry from one college to another, trying to catch what people are saying through the silence of one field path and then another and another, first pushing as if wading through crowds and then being suddenly alone, as he thought he wanted to be, only to find he could not stand the solitude and never once saying to himself the few words of admission, that he might have been the cause, that he *was* the cause. These words, even as a question, which would have been an alleviation.

As he walks now, he remembers returning then at nightfall only to resume his solitary walking the next day. His pain made worse by remembered pleasure. They had shared the sky and the earth, the horse chestnuts and the silver birches, liking together the ice-cold beauty of buildings and trees, fragile in the clear freshness of the early morning. Kings College, serene with benediction, an unreachable Goddess, they declared every time, unreachable in the private knowledge, the inheritance of thought and belief, enclosed in the perfection of silk-smooth stone and stained glass. There was too, later, a curious form of consolation, a reprieve. This was in the comparison he made. He compared, in detail, the handsome young lovers with the smooth, sun-bronzed and athletic bodies of the warriors in the mythology of Ancient Greece and was, in this way, able to look upon the deaths as the fulfilment of a predicted fate which, after drawing him in, had left him out. It seemed simple then to be left out of someone else's destiny even when he acknowledged that his own destiny, in being inadvertently followed, apparently caused destruction elsewhere. One of them, himself included, could have died from an illness, a heart attack or an accident at any time.

But this death, their death, their leap enfolded, was not that same sort of death.

Not dying, he was bereaved, he mourned. He was the mourner for himself.

୭

Returning now, as he does at night, to Mrs Porter's with the fear of even more unwanted memories and regrets, he does not try to stop the expected recollection of the bitter humiliation in the name of therapy and cure during which he was obliged to force himself, crouched and weeping, grovelling to disclose and betray as something evil the only good and, to him, the sweetest thing in his life.

The shuffling in the leaves and twigs behind him causes him to feel that he is being followed. His distaste cancels any fear of the sinister. He is ashamed of this distaste, which is heightened by the thought that, yet again, he is being followed by his fellow lodgers. The sickly waiter and his suspected infection (a disease more dreaded since its relentless and secret progress becomes more evident) will not be alone. Dalton is sure that Perce will be with him. The two are always, in some terrible way, together. Treading, even more lightly, he listens for the continued disturbance on the path, but all is silent. Either they have turned aside or they are

99

waiting till he is gone from them. Meanwhile, as he walks, Mrs Porter's place creeps in its unwanted bulk towards him.

As he so often does, he turns his thoughts to remembering the more constructive threads of discussion which, in confrontation with a certain kind of ignorance, were enlightening. He remembers clearly his own attempt to reason the unmentionable leap, the leap made by the two lovers, into some kind of proportion. During discussions at Cambridge the thought persisted that if you influence someone, you give them something intangible and precious which is yours. You give them a sensitivity, a wisdom, perhaps a tenderness, something exquisite which they did not have before. Once under such an influence, the other person becomes someone else.

Can a child, he remembers someone asking, can a child influence, to this extent, an adult? Is an inexperienced adult, someone else questioned, anything more than a child? The great thing emerging from the confusion of ideas was the acknowledgement that the need was to develop and to understand oneself and to make allowance for, in this development, the passions. Once this freedom of attitude disappeared, it seemed to Dalton, during his rehabilitation, that most people were afraid and would not have the courage to be what they were. And, they would not then be able to consider the ultimate value of beauty, the enjoyment of beauty and the joy of human companionship. Especially they would not be aware of their own beauty in youth and the effect of this beauty on someone else. Then there was the excitement and the nourishing to be had from literature. Dalton remembers his own desire for intellectual and emotional intimacy and he, without wanting to, thinks about the hundred books he set himself to read during his first year at university.

Cornelius had beauty. Dalton stands still under the dark trees pausing with this intrusion of thought. Cornelius during the evening had come, wrapped in a bath towel, to the small bathroom which opened off the conservatory where Dalton was sitting, still wearing his raincoat, beside the low folding bed which had, as usual, been made up for him.

Cornelius, with many flourishings of the patterned edges of his towel, explained that the upstairs bathroom would be occupied for at least two hours.

'Ursula, of course,' he said, 'steam and perfume.' Throwing his towel into the fronds of some miniature palm trees he began to recite: *Only see, he has all the terrible beauty of the Greek tragedy,* how does it go on? *And still he is not wounded and not killed.* He said he thought it was a misquotation and, in any case, he did not know who wrote it. He crouched, with both taps on, mixing the hot and cold water. Standing up in the bath he addressed Dalton with a long speech about his mother and her friends who were preparing to spend the night, even in all the wind and the rain, sleeping in old newspapers and cardboard boxes on the benches in the park. It was a protest, a statement, he explained, and they were hoping to raise money for a shelter for people who had nowhere to go, street kids, he said, and bag women.

In his indignation, still standing in the steaming bath, Cornelius had wept, saying that there were other ways of providing a house for people, who had no home, to sleep in. Dalton not knowing how, in words or actions, to reconcile himself and the frail boy to the unexpected actions of these well-meaning people, thought of one thing only and that was that he should leave at once. He should leave Cornelius in his nakedness. He made for the door, knocking over an erect and correct little palm, breaking the slender container and clumsily spilling the rich damp earth over the clean tiles.

'In any case,' Cornelius cried out after him, 'mother has plenty of money. She could give them some money. She shouldn't sleep in a box in the rain. Sleeping in boxes is just something for show.' And then he cried, a long wailing cry, begging Dalton not to leave.

❧

Contemplating later, as he walks, the tears which seemed to splash from the boy's eyes, and remembering perhaps too much, the white skin which contained the thin body, Dalton wished he had not heard the boy calling him back to share the hot water and reminding him that his bed in the ferns was made up ready for him. Not knowing what he should do, acting as he often did without making a decision, he walked as quickly and as lightly as he could away down the side path to the road.

It was the same thing all over again. Dalton had known, and Greyhead had known, that the treatment, the rehabilitation, had not changed him in any way. And that was why he had undergone the so-called treatment more than once. Now having left Cornelius weeping, and the whole house probably hearing this weeping, Dalton recalls others who had wept in his presence, not wanting to be left and, at the same time, afraid of the consequences if not left. He knew that the only possibility was to walk away.

The much disputed question of homosexuality, Morrison the Master of Music at Cambridge, he of the ardent and sustained voice, would say during a brief rest in the middle of the long hours of choral practice, the much disputed question was thought to be an idealistic admiration between an adult man and an attractive youth with a degree of initiation, experience and understanding, enriching them both.

Dalton thinks, as he walks, about Morrison and his easy way of saying things, easy because they were a part of his whole well-thought-out way of being. Morrison never said anything without consideration. He had, within him, a core of sound belief from which he could always offer an opinion or question someone else's opinion. His singing came from this same core. Dalton remembers the Bach Cantata, *Ich hatte viel Bekümmernis*. In response to the pure soprano of the boy's voice, *Komm mein Jesu, und erquicke* ... Morrison's voice, vibrant with intense feeling, replied with an unforgettable ardour which stirred the deepest of deep feeling, *Ja, ach ja, ich liebe dich! Entweichet, ihr sorgen, verschwinde, du Schmerze* ...

Dalton, at that time, singing in his turn, the tenor part; *Erfreue dich, Seele erfreue dich, Herze* ... experienced, as if felt in his heart, the erotic, the sexual awakening which is a part of the deep sensual and intellectual, the complete satisfaction to be felt in music.

Dalton has learned, during subsequent years to take consolation in thinking of Morrison and in remembering Morrison's explanation. He, within shouting distance now of Mrs Porter's place, slows his pace to think of the Ancient Greeks who considered the delicate idealistic attachment as being necessary and, in some ways, possibly superior to the love between a man and a woman. He even allows himself the fleeting memory of listening to the boy singing when they, the two of them, were alone that time immediately before the interruption. As well as listening, Dalton, leaning forward to the boy, sang gently in reply from that voice described as sustained and ardent, he sang in turn, *Ja, ach ja, ich liebe dich!*

The precious friendship, described by Morrison, was noble, impassioned and romantic, and it included the whole sense of the intellectual and the spiritual purity, and could only be realised through the passions of reverence and pity and awe. All this, he has to understand, could be, with fear of self-recognition and contemporary ignorance, completely degraded and destroyed. Dalton recalls, in the dark, in the fringes of the city, his own reading and he dwells for a few minutes on the idea of the spiritual and the emotional catharsis which is aesthetic and not simply a moral issue. Such idealism seems to be entirely beyond his reach in spite of all his reading. He shivers, without meaning to, at the thought of the kind of scene which might have followed if he had taken off his clothes and stepped into the bath with Cornelius. Having this thought is a part of the conditioning undertaken in the rehabilitation. It is the turning away from the desired moment. The rehabilitation officer, the grey-haired, rosy-faced man called it *being sensible* or *being watchful.*

Be on your guard, he said to Dalton that day, when Dalton left with his case and his raincoat. Dalton knows he is making the picture now, after the event, of the kind of interruption which might have taken place if he had stayed.

Cornelius, he expects, is merely playing, acting a part in order to hide the compelling attraction between the brother and the sister. Or it might be simply, because they were being regarded still as children, they were bored. Dalton, in imagination, likes to believe that the ultimate and exquisite secret is between the two, a desire nurtured and kept alive.

Cornelius's life, enviable as it might be, is like his embroidery, the tapestry occupying the end wall in the room they call the library, unfinished, dark in places, the silks knotted and frayed with some squares of canvas too heavily covered and others lacking stitches and colour. It is an unfinished pretence, strangled as Cornelius himself is strangled, in the floral glazed cotton of the chair coverings, in the restrictions imposed by an unfeeling and frightened society, and last and by no means least, in the family in which he wordlessly finds himself. There is something else too in Dalton's own wordless perception, he can see that Cornelius suffers, without being able to explain to himself, the edges of his mother's deep unhappiness. He supposes that, in some measure, all sons are capable of this. He thinks of the man, father, Consul and husband. He is a small vivacious man, his short pointed beard juts from his chin adding to the expression of eagerness for every experience but, in particular, an eagerness for music, for precision in performance and completeness in listening. His eyes are small and bright and penetrating. Dalton has not seen him since the first meeting when he was, with lavish gestures and words, made welcome and, at once, invited to contribute to the *chamber music en famille.* The Consul had reminded Dalton then that he knew from the authorities of his particular abilities in the cantata. It was like the Consul, a certain kind of man, Dalton thought then, to mention *the authorities,* seeming to push him, at once, into a category wherein he was meant to be kept.

The woman, the woman, the wife of the Consul, the mother of Ursula and Cornelius (the father must have chosen these names) with her loud, friendly voice and her jokes, her sixth-form English schoolgirl accent and language, which she brought back with her to Australia, would have given aunt Dalton and his mother something to laugh over. She was quite different from her husband. In comparison she seemed to lack the qualities of the kind of person who would take pleasure in a cultured approach to reading and discussion or even letter writing. She would have no real desire, Dalton could not quite explain it to himself, he thought she would have no honest desire for intellectual and emotional intimacy but, he felt, that as these were expected from her, she would do her best to produce them. Dalton does not speak of it simply because he does not speak of anything.

It is not difficult for Dalton to imagine the Consul's wife and her friends shrieking with jokes and laughter in the rain as they try to fit themselves into plastic bags and cardboard boxes for the night.

All the same, without ever really having a conversation with her, he knows that he likes her. For hasn't she, without any questions, been very kind to him? And, however mad the idea might seem to an ordinary person, the fact remains that these women, used to luxury, will be very uncomfortable for the night and are doing this because they really feel, in their hearts, the human plight of being without bed and without food and shelter every night. Dalton, in a moment of truthful self-examination, knows that he is not prepared, on behalf of others, to spend a night in the cold as the Consul's wife will be doing.

Dalton knows that in trying secretly, at some time, to emulate the admired writers he must take part in the pursuit of truth. On reflection he understands perfectly that he is quite unable to bring the past into the present, especially for the two young people. He is unable to provide the kind of wisdom and friendship which would surround them with the happy and moral environment they need. Monsieur Perdu might perhaps, but he is inclined to move only in small unintentional circles, pausing for the occasional pirouette, as he keeps close to the soft folds of the clinging marocain dress and, at the same time, seeming to be blamelessly unaware of the comfortable flesh nestling within. M. Perdu is, without doubt, the suitable companion for Cornelius and Dalton must remember, thankfully, Greyhead's thoughtful and timely advice.

The boy, at that time, reminded Dalton of other boys. He was reminded of the sweet accents and the treble voices in the part of the school choir consisting entirely of the little boys. It was in particular this one boy, later, singing solo, and the evident effort he made to achieve the exact fall in cadence after maintaining the single high note in the necessary measured sequence. It always seemed to Dalton that it was as if the entire choir, in their accompanying silence, held the notes voiceless as they, waiting, held their own breathing while the child brought his own voice down through the change of key with such perfection.

The boy, at that time (in the university choir), was in his infancy, like a sprig from a special and rare herb waiting, in innocence, to be gathered. The idea of a fragile green stem and the tiny curled leaves, fresh and unspoiled, still growing, was appealing beyond reason. The boy had come, still in his surplice, following him to his door. When Dalton opened the door, the child was waiting outside. And, when he moved away, he turned to look back as if his movement, in the face of Dalton's questioning frown, was an invitation.

It was when he followed the child back into the calm,

sun-filled shaft of colour directly below the holy window that he was discovered.

Instead of remaining, kneeling where he was, leaning forward towards the boy, listening to the clear youthful soprano rising as if in justification of the childish presumption in the unspoken invitation, Dalton, filled with feelings of worship, stood up and moved towards the child, altering his own voice to the deeper tone for the words; *Ja, ach ja, ich liebe dich!* He sensed the intrusion, rather than seeing the two men. He, half turning, left immediately, running in long quiet strides, without attempting to meet the intruders with any kind of explanation. This too, in the rehabilitation, the 'cure', should have been unwrapped and brought to some logical explained conclusion. The admission of a wish. The response to an invitation. A forbidden invitation, sweet and carrying danger in its sweetness.

During the years of the journey through conflict and repetitions of treatment, he came to the understanding that the child had observed and sensed the magic and the beauty of desire and attraction, and already understood that there was a special perception of this, which he possessed, and was seeking the complete satisfaction in the music which was matched in the playful tenderness of touch and embrace.

During his long journey Dalton came to know, in

advance, how the hard eyes in the world to which he must ultimately return, could change to an unforgiving softness which failed to hide both curiosity and accusation.

Dalton never described to anyone his pleasure in the sweet, clear purity of the child's voice and the love the child expressed, in his eyes, for the tenderness in the deep reply. He, Dalton, never once allowed himself the justification of speaking about the invitation which was in the boy's reluctant step and the backward glance. He protected, for ever, both the sound and the look.

Sometimes when Dalton is walking he is overtaken with grief. He is afraid of being mad with grief, mad in the grief and the emptiness. He has no reason for being alive and is afraid of the futility which accompanies this lack of reason. If he thinks of the boy, of the expression in his youthful and loving eyes, and the way in which the sunlight through the holy window blessed the boy's sweet head, he has to tell himself that the child will now be fully grown to manhood, perhaps muscular, even coarse and thick set instead of the slender little creature he was. He might well be the kind of man for whom it would be impossible to write a poem or even a letter.

What is your father like? Do you talk to your father? Does your father talk to you? Is your father alive? If he is dead what do you remember most about him? All these questions then about his father and himself. At the time it was not too difficult to say, because all the other men, in turn, were saying in the language they were being taught to use: 'My father and I did not communicate.' And when asked why not, the answer was, every time, a studied helpless shrug and the words, 'I don't know,' said almost out of hearing. Remembering his father removing the remains of a boiled egg from the breakfast table, Dalton, every time wanted to cry out: 'But I think of my father. I think of him.' Forgetting the scorn and distaste, he wanted his father when it was too late, and when he was unable to say just once to him the words which would have made all the difference.

'Choose a book, Dalton,' his father said one day when they were alone together in a bookshop which kept open on Sunday afternoons. 'Choose a book,' he said, 'choose any book you'd like.' They stood, father and son, close together uneasily among people who seemed to know all about books and which particular ones they wanted. Children with clever eyes were choosing too. Young Dalton watched them. He heard a boy, older than he was, scoffing. He followed at a respectful distance as this handsome boy moved, with a thoughtful expression, from the Children's Section towards Modern Adult Fiction and on to Classics. His father followed.

'These are nice books,' his father said. 'Dalton, take a look at these, these are very nice. Good bindings. See? The bindings.' His father handled a book so Dalton handled one too. The cover, soft as if the cherished contents were pillowed in an unseen layer of swans' down, was pleasant to hold. Title and author were embossed richly in gold in the mulberry-coloured leather.

'*Treasure Island*, Dalton,' his father's voice was both eager and reverent. '*Treasure Island*, I'll bet that's a good tale.'

Dalton, choosing *Treasure Island*, carried it home in a brown paper bag. Surreptitiously, at home, discovering that he could not read it, he opened the book in several places, sniffing at its newness with a secret pleasure.

'*Treasure Island*?' His mother and aunt Dalton were shown the book in the evening while his father looked on. 'But Dalton, Darling! You should have chosen something else.' His mother gave him a fond little shake. 'We already have this one in the set with *Black Beauty*, *Robinson Crusoe*, *Alice* and all the rest of them ...' She waved an arm towards the bookshelves.

'It doesn't matter,' his father said then, and he went

on to explain that the books they already had were old and out of date, printed a long time ago and not as good as this newly printed one would be.

Aunt Dalton and his mother raised their eyebrows at each other. They shrugged their shoulders in mock despair and his mother, clutching her mouth, rushed from the room. Dalton, recognizing the symptoms of the held-down laugh, understood at once that his father's remark was that of an uneducated person, a Horsefly. And later, when his father offered to read the first few pages of the new book with him to 'get him into the story', Dalton told him that he was sorry, he was too busy ...

Contribution from Mrs M. Disley

It's no use you standing on the seat
The crabs in here can jump six feet

It's no use you going in next door
The crabs in there jump six feet four.

Dalton Foster letting himself in at Mrs Porter's front door discovers Miss Mallow waiting for him in her half-open doorway. She is dressed in a long garment made of thin material which, Dalton notices at once, is not at all warm enough.

'Oh, Mr Afton,' Miss Mallow scarcely seems to do more than breathe the words across the poorly lighted hall.

'Foster,' Dalton says with his small sideways smile. To his embarrassment Miss Mallow detains him with her cold hand.

'Oh, yes, of course, Mr Foster,' Miss Mallow corrects herself. 'I do forget things so easily. Did you know,' she continues, 'that Clementi, the father of the modern pianoforte, was, in the first place, adopted by his teacher and became a child prodigy and then, later on, he was turned out of the house by his teacher who said he, Clementi, should be *castrated?* I have often wondered,' Miss Mallow ventures a step further into the hall, 'I have often wondered whose wife he stole.' Dalton, about to go upstairs, pauses at the foot of the stairs. It seems impolite to move away at once.

'I would like, Mr Afton,' Miss Mallow's thin face is

flushed, 'I would like Mrs Afton to know, Mr Afton, that I never thought once of stealing you from her. My main thought, you know Mr Afton, is that my piano, which you gave me when we packed up the school, resembles in some small way the instrument which Clementi, the master, created and played himself.'

'Yes, yes, of course.' Dalton has only the smallest words to give in response.

'Mr Afton, please do you think, could I have dinner in my room? Would you order a little dinner, just something on a tray, for me and, perhaps, a very small whisky and water? Thank you so much.' Miss Mallow, clutching the thin grey cobwebs of her dress to her chest, backs into her room. She closes her door and, opening it once more, leans forward, nodding and smiling, saying, 'A Bientôt,' putting one finger to her lips as if to guard their secret.

Dalton starts to go slowly upstairs to his room. He is hardly able to bear the thought of this starved, sad woman alone in her cold room, waiting for a drink and a dinner which will never arrive. Later he would hear her playing the piano for a short time before she, after a long pause, would close the lid. Why ever had he walked away from the house? Away from Cornelius? His bath, after all, was hardly a threat. He would have long finished his bath by now. Perhaps he should return to the house. He was expected there, his bed was already made up for him in the conservatory. He should have stayed as arranged. Hardly staying more than a few minutes in his room, he comes out once more, uneasily, on to the landing.

A sound on the stairs from above causes Winch to draw Dalton into the doorway of the room he shares with Perce. Dalton, who had not known that Perce and Winch were in, is surprised. He had not heard them come home.

'It's the floor show in drag,' Winch says, letting go of Dalton's arm. 'It's the floor show, they'll come down in the act, they'll keep it up all the way along the road to the hotel. It's the mood,' he says, 'it's to get the mood up, they have to get it up and keep it that way till they get down there. It's the mood, see. Four nights a week, they do, they have to keep it up four nights.'

Dalton wonders how Perce and Winch, after dropping behind during the dark walk, can be here so quickly. He thinks too of the empty way to the corner, the fenced-off railway line on one side and the squat hostel next door with all the lights extinguished before eight o'clock every evening, and further along, the sinister unremovable foundations of a demolished factory. The pools of stagnant water never drain completely away from this desolate place.

These boys upstairs back, the ones called Pootsie, Trotter and Slem, there will be no one out there in the street to see the synchronised rhythm and grace of the three pretty boys, and perhaps no one very much in the bar of the hotel to admire and applaud.

So far, the boys, Pootsie, Trotter and Slem, have never so much as glanced at Dalton. Even so, their curls, their ear-rings and their gaudy faces frighten him. One of them might even put out an audacious hand to touch him in passing.

Slem, he understands, is probably slim, Perce has this way of speaking in which pink becomes penk and milk is melk and Winch is Wench ... He is nervous of them too.

In his moment of fear which does not pass easily Dalton tries to recall the attitude of the Greeks towards fate; on leaving the Centre he made a resolution in silence, to calmly defy and, at the same time, accept the inevitable, whatever his destiny would be. He would have no fear, but always accept challenge and reconcili-ation, and regard what might lie ahead for him as the Greeks did, with a *mixture of defiance and resignation*. The pretty boys may well have no hand in what was in store for him. He imagines their progress to the corner. He has known many dreary ways to dreary corners, the ways to schools, to prisons, to courtrooms, to cemeteries and to Mrs Porter's. Perhaps this last one is the worst. He has, after all, come out from his room for no other reason than to escape from it. If he is able to be truthful to himself, he wants to escape from his thoughts and the voices — the remembered anxiety in his mother's voice when she told aunt Dalton, one evening, that she felt it was a sinister thing when a certain slack-mouthed, cold-lipped, self-absorbed man known to them both as *Lover Boy* enquired: 'And how is young Dalton these days?'

'But Darling!' aunt Dalton, as usual, had her own remedy; 'so many adjectives, that lover, that paramour manque, that *creature* does not deserve them.'

Dalton, awake from this sleepless nightmare, feeling as if from an infection the ache of Flaubert's deep and secret wound, wishes for the enclosed poetic world of the imagination, he wishes for companionship and beauty instead of the ugly and the sinister. He is surprised to understand that he needs the transient company of Perce and Winch on their shared landing, this place where the stairs turn and continue on upwards towards the back of the house, and then on and up another flight to the pretty boys where they rest, during the day, in their boudoir. He cringes, while trying not to, towards Perce and Winch as the boys pass, each with a hand raised to the shoulder of the one in front, the leader, also with his hand raised and his elbow bent, causing him to resemble a particular kind of water bird reminiscent of imitations in plaster of Paris, stained and chipped with unwanted experience.

In the hall downstairs, Dalton pauses unable to make up his mind about going out once more into the night. He can hear the flat notes of Miss Mallow's piano. She is, he thinks, probably working her way through the one hundred études of Clementi; the *Gradus ad Parnassum*, declaring at intervals to the emptiness of her room that the art of modern piano playing is derived from these studies. And she would add, in her soft voice, an explanation that, in spite of the accusation levelled against him, or because of it, Clementi had qualities which were genuine and, her voice gaining more than usual strength, she would announce to the sad walls of her room that she did hope that she was reproducing in some small measure some of the splendid quality of his music on her own instrument.

To think of Miss Mallow in detail is to consider Mr Afton himself, pale, freckled, a kind, white-haired old man who was once a pale, freckled schoolboy, responsible in authority as ink monitor. On his arrival in the classroom the teacher, nodding permission would wait, his smooth pointer midway between desk top and the world, shining high up, unrolled, the map covering the length of the blackboard, while the ink monitor, without spilling a drop, filled the ink wells. Piano tuner and teacher of the pianoforte, later, Mr Afton was offered a country school where, as headmaster, he played the piano for the hymn every morning and Miss Mallow, in pale clinging dresses, sat beside him turning the pages. It was impossible to imagine that this quiet and gentle man had been obliged to retire from his position because of an accusation made against him, and which was found to be untrue, but not until his name had been, as Miss Mallow put it, shamefully dragged through the newspapers. 'People,' Miss Mallow on one occasion said to Dalton, 'people love indecency and repeat what they have read in the newspapers and, naturally, they require a victim. And the victim becomes the reason and the explanation for them for what has gone wrong in their own families.' She wiped away her tears and said she was sorry to talk so much. Mr Afton's heart was broken, she said.

Indecision. Animals actually die because of being undecided, the thought comes to him as he stands with one foot on the first tread of the stairs. Indecision. It is late to be setting out to walk back to the house even if his room at Mrs Porter's is unapproachable, packed as it is with thoughts and remarks abandoned there, wandering and restless and sad, waiting for his return.

He supposes it is far too late now to hope that the door of the conservatory has been left open for him.

But this thing about animals, he has read, somewhere, of experiments carried out on rabbits. They were subjected to choice, and unable to make a choice, unable to decide, they starved to death. He wonders where he read this. It seems to be more like something which Winch would know about, from a newspaper or in his excited reporting from his evening class. Without choosing, Dalton, with slow and careful steps, makes his way back up to his room. He will try and think about rabbits in relation to human behaviour rather than Miss Mallow's heart-breaking memories and thoughts of Mr Afton.

There were people, he tells himself, who enjoy other people's misfortunes. Miss Mallow could well be, in other hands, the recipient of *Schadenfreude*.

Mornings and evenings he walks. Whole days he walks. He walks either on the fringes of the city keeping near the railway yards and the markets, or he follows the quiet streets in the leafy suburb, drawn irresistibly to the house and the two young people and their tutor. Often he pauses in the park which is usually deserted. Seen from a little distance, as he approaches, it is as if the park, deeply green, is submerged in clear tranquil water.

Dalton stops at a greengrocer's shop on the way to the park. It is an unusual shop, old fashioned, reminding him of shops long ago, in England, where baskets and tubs of fruit and vegetables were displayed on the footpath in front of the window. Poultry hung then, as it was the custom, suspended high up, reachable only with a special pole which had a hook on the end. It is not difficult to recall the rumpled brown feathers, the engorged dark colour of the combs and the dirty yellow feet crossed and tied together for hanging.

With the apples, in a small bag, in his raincoat pocket he thinks of the pleasure of seeing the thin, hungry, little girl being pleased to receive them. He remembers part of a poem;

> *A glimmering girl*
> *With apple blossom in her hair*

He will carry the apples with him everywhere.

Headline: SCHOOL PRINCIPAL BEATS WIFE
               WITH GARDEN HOSE

Mrs Porter: I don't doubt she needed it. The Brazen
               Hussy. Probbley lorst his job. Lorst his school
               and all.
                   I'll lay a bet *she* had something rolling ...

MENU 4 2 NITE

Roast of Pork apple soss
Roasted Potatoes
Cabbage
Bread and Butter Pudding
Bingo: Tea or coffee.

Mrs Porter: Love blows hot and love blows cold
               Give yourself a treat EV a new
               hair do, a manicure, a bubble bath.
               Mr Right might be slow. But,
               Time is ON YOUR SIDE.

Afraid of meeting Miss Mallow in the hall, Dalton Foster is furtive on the stairs, curling his toes in his shoes, hoping to avoid creaking boards. On the landing too he treads lightly. He does not want Perce and Winch to know when he comes in and when he goes out. Every day he tries to be as quiet as possible.

Miss Mallow, as if she has been waiting for Dalton, comes out of her room the moment he steps in off the pavement. It is the end of the afternoon and the evening will be a cold one. The mist is already rising from the long grass along the fence by the railway line.

'Mr Afton,' Miss Mallow says, 'Mr Afton, I wonder …'

'Foster,' Dalton, pausing just inside the front door, corrects her. 'Foster.'

'Oh, Mr Foster, I do beg your pardon.' Miss Mallow, hovering and uncertain, puts a hand on his sleeve. 'I tell Mr Afton everything. You see, I was with him right up to the time the school closed. That dreadful accusation … you know. I feel sure he can hear me so I talk to him, all the time – but I am detaining you and it is possible that I have told you this before. You see, I feel that Mrs Porter, though I am perhaps a little more refined and educated, I always feel that Mrs Porter, because of being a widow, has managed – knows she has managed something more in her life, that is, she has been married to Mr Porter. Miss Vales, you know, said this outright, you know, she said: "Being a widow, means that she's done something you and I haven't managed to do. She's found Mr Right. True she lost him, but before that she found him and that's more than I shall ever do." Miss Vales, she cried terribly and I said, "Oh please don't, Miss Vales, please don't cry."'

Dalton nods and gulps and steps towards the stairs.

'Please do have this, Mr Foster.' Miss Mallow presses a small box into his unwilling hand. 'It's called Balm of Roses,' she says. 'I hope you don't mind accepting a stolen article.' She pauses. 'I never thought I would be a thief. I thought it was a packet of cheese – you know how we have to find our own supper – and this must have been in the wrong place on the shelves, or else I was in a different part of the shop. The supermarket is so huge and I don't see at all well, especially when I'm being a thief, you know, when I am stealing something.'

'Most kind of you,' Dalton mutters, slipping the little package into his raincoat pocket. He clears his throat and climbs the stairs two at a time.

❦

The floorboards on the landing creak. Perce and Winch, having a discussion, come out from their room. Winch is trying to explain to Perce about something he calls the Dootchablick.

'It's German,' he says. 'It's German,' he says to Dalton. 'Mr Foster,' he says, 'I'm telling Perce here about the *stare*, the German *stare*, the way the Germans *stare* ahead not noticing what's going on. I've been reading about it, it's what happens when people is indifferent to all that's happening. Apathy it's called, it's all round us. The Germans had this Dootchablick and that's how Hitler got on up where he got to.'

'Too Right, Wench,' Perce says in a soothing voice.

'It's what he's learning at Night School,' Perce apologises. 'Hit's Hokay, Wench old man, the gentleman's going back out again, let him pass.' Perce draws Winch into the doorway of their room.

'At this time of night?' Winch pretends to consult a wristwatch, squinting at Dalton sideways as he does so. 'The gentleman's only just come home, he'll want to freshen up.'

'Come on, Wench.' Perce drags at his jacket. 'Let our gentleman pass ... He's had a bit more education than he's ready for,' Perce explains, with a wink, to Dalton. Dalton, when the way is clear, avoiding their eyes, immediately runs back downstairs without going into his room at all.

The Balm of Roses will make a nice present for someone. For Ursula, at the house, or better still, for the little girl, if he can find her, as he hopes, playing alone in the park. Smiling because of this thought, he gives a small wave upwards towards the first landing and, with some difficulty, forces open the swollen front door.

The apples, he thought at the time when he bought them, were poetic fruits. They were and are: *the golden apples of the Sun*. He looks forward now to the way in which she will hold her small grateful hands to receive his gift. She may well be in the park even at this late hour. She may even sleep there. A hopeful thought.

As he walks Dalton reflects on the kind of difference there could be in Miss Mallow's life if she had a friend. Not simply any kind of friend but a woman who would meet Miss Mallow's tear-filled eyes with a steady look, at once tender and serious. A woman's gaze in which the beauty would be this serious tenderness. Any awkwardness of nose and chin and any haggard quality, resulting from painful and secret experience, would be outweighed by the expression in the eyes. Everything could be changed for Miss Mallow by the exchanging of a look or an arching of the eyebrows. There would be the voice too. As in a Beethoven sonata for cello and piano, the voice, like the cello, would be tremulous and sustained and, at the same time, both pleading and reassuring. At times, contained in the voice, there would be a dance and, at other times, a lullaby, caressing and consoling. The cello suggests, as Dalton recalls the sonata, the more earnest side of the friendship which would have made her life completely different. For one thing she would not, at this time in her life, be alone in a damp, downstairs room overlooking a dismal street and with an almost derelict piano which she either fails, or refuses, to see is in this pathetic condition.

There would be no mischief in the relationship, for example the mischief generated, without shame, by his mother as she flew from one room to the next pursued by aunt Dalton. Miss Mallow's friend suggests rather, the cellist leaning slightly towards the pianist, whose glance turns with approval, and hoped for approval, to the cellist. Both Miss Mallow and her friend would be mysterious in their dress, somewhat shabby in their drapery and wearing their hair looped under forward-dipping hats. Both would have a tendency to dark circles round the eyes which have, in their soft gaze, sleeplessness. There would be an intimacy, a shared responsibility.

They would tell each other if their slips were showing and they would dust off each other's excess talcum powder.

There would be remembered and repeated conversations, thoughts and images which would sustain, perhaps a cathedral lantern, the only one of its kind in England, ecclesiastical, high up in the roof wonderfully light and awesome. She would be able to think, with a small smile of tender recollection of a journey on a river boat, a crested grebe alone on the grass close to the water's edge not moving as the boat passes to float on between two long fields of flax in deep blue flower. And on the boat, while knowing her friend is seeing and feeling all that she is feeling and seeing, on the boat she could simply sit, watching four women passing one piece of knitting from one to another, during the pauses at the lock gates, each one taking a turn, unrolling the wool a little more, with the knitting needles in constant movement.

Mr Afton, Miss Mallow's single possession, her old headmaster with whom she worked, might have had the same necessary qualities which belong to the idea of a woman friend. He might have had a womanly sensitivity and a cultural perception matching Miss Mallow's needs. And there would have existed between them a friendship without any sexual challenge.

During these thoughts Dalton scarcely notices the

distance and the darkness. He has become accustomed to this freedom of walking and being overtaken by his thoughts and by the blackness which covers the trees, the grass, the gardens and the houses adding to the silence in the suburb as, gradually, the soft roar of the ever wakeful city is left behind, subdued.

On this night the moon is racing up the sky. Already the roof tops, touched by moonlight, give an impression of being snow covered. Moonlight and shadow cast a pattern, a trellis of branches as if dropped and scattered over the surface of the road. He caresses the apples nestled deep in his pocket and feels confident that, this time, he will find the little girl in the park. Because of her appearance he knows that she has nowhere to go. There is no one waiting for her, expecting her to return. He is warm with the hope of finding her. He is quite prepared to share the little girl with Miss Mallow. It might be necessary to accept advice from Miss Mallow because of the things which can only be spoken about by a woman to a young girl as she approaches womanhood. At this thought he experiences a small hidden thrill of excitement. He stops before he reaches the park and, turning the corner, he follows the road to the house. In putting off the pleasure of finding the child, his happiness will be increased with the anticipation of the meeting.

'I've always made a point of choosing men friends whose mothers are already dead.' Dalton, pausing in the clinical light of the porch, his finger almost on the bell, can hear the Consul's wife, in her rich telephone voice, advising as she often does. In the distance beyond the voice, someone, Ursula most probably, is playing the piano, practising, stopping in the middle of a phrase and starting again. Cornelius, Dalton feels sure, will be leaning in the doorway with his embroidery limp and trailing, or he might, in a different mood altogether, be sitting with a certain formal grace at his tapestry, an unusual hunting scene depicting an imaginary reconstruction of the woods near Vienna with the silent huntsmen, downcast, approaching the Hunting Lodge at Mayerling immediately after receiving the news of the suicide of Crown Prince Rudolph and Maria Vetsera.

Dalton stands to one side of the porch, a stranger in the shadow, standing still, not ringing the door bell. He, lacking position in the family and in society itself, listens greedily to the sounds of the family. He hears their laughter and then more laughter and he understands once more that he can never really know these other people. They live in such close obligation to one another. He is excluded even from obligation, which, though carrying responsibility, brings enrichment and pleasure, often unexpected. He knows the room where the two young people will be sitting. This room is like a left-over room in an old university, a study for a professor, perhaps a man who loved poetry. The windows are tall and narrow. The room itself is large and warm with walls of books, a forgotten library, a strange unmatching mixture of books chosen and studied by someone over a great many years and then forsaken, no longer wanted. On his first visit to the house the Consul's wife had said to him to 'browse and borrow'. He had been too timid, in spite of an inclination, to take advantage.

Ursula and Cornelius, at eighteen and sixteen, seem too grown up for the services of a tutor. Dalton envies the tutor; his place is desirable. Putting himself in that place, at times, he has asked himself what could he teach these two special children. He could describe for them something of the noble philosophy which was inseparable from the golden beauty of the naked young men engaged in wrestling or in dancing in the palaestra as they, performing for each other, achieved perfect precision in the movements required for their skill as warriors.

Or, he could read poetry of course;

> And someone called me by my name:
> It had become a glimmering girl

With apple blossom in her hair ...
I will find out where she has gone,
And kiss her lips and take her hands;
And walk among long dappled grass,
And pluck till time and times are done
The silver apples of the moon,
The golden apples of the sun.

If he lived in this house, if he had a room here, perhaps the particular one with the gable windows from which he could look right into the surrounding trees, he would be free from the burden of his thoughts and his intention *and* his subsequent return to Mrs Porter's establishment. He would, in fact, be someone else and would be living without his present sadness and fear. There is always the thought that another place will offer a different life. The sudden return to the present truth about his life really comes about by the understanding that the thought, unspeakable and unspoken, must remain with its owner and, if necessary, be kept there until death.

To continue with the picture of himself in the desired place of tutor he easily sees his own feet in good-quality leather slippers, the heels walked on and pressed down. It is only a small step to seeing himself left in charge while the music-loving Consul and his fashionable wife are away in Europe pursuing Art and other Consuls and their fashionable wives. All, at once, it is the day of the expected return and there is great activity. Cornelius will apply himself to his dreary tapestry, Ursula will squeal on her violin with diligence and, as a gesture, there he will be, himself, standing at the lectern with pens and ink, demonstrating his skill in calligraphy, copying out, in German, a poem of welcome or a suitable passage of prose on the subject of homecoming, from Goethe or from Thomas Mann, well spaced on the page and decorated with pressed flowers.

The whole scene, he knows, is fantastic and impossible.

❧

He knows that if he rings the bell he will be invited indoors for supper, buttered sugar loaf and a glass of cold milk, in comfort by the fire in the library. Ursula, laughing, might play the piano or her violin, even inventing a musical joke with one of the instruments. Cornelius, his medieval embroidery, as always, attached by a braid or a ribbon to his thin wrist, will lean over the back of a chair reading aloud, paraphrasing as he reads, insisting that it is delicious to be tempted, that destiny is cruel and sends no warnings, that ultimately there is no choice and no freedom, at certain times, to exercise the will, and that it is impossible to contemplate consequences. So familiar is Dalton with this reminder of his own undergradute ideas that it would be easy for him to counter, in his mind only of course, these thoughts with remarks which become equal in discussion. He could recite easily that blackmail often has no trustworthy evidence, that, mostly, self creation exists in the imagination and that all individuals have problems for which there are no solutions.

When faced with Cornelius and his arguments, Dalton does not reply with knowledge and experience from his own reading. He merely nods his head, gazing at the boy and thinking, in his silence, that should he have the privilege of being the tutor to Cornelius, he could provide many other avenues of philosophical thought.

He is unable to press the bell. His finger caresses the central spot as if with longing. He knows he is always kindly, if mockingly, received by these children. To them he is forever the DP, the displaced person, the homeless person to whom hospitality must be shown. He knows that their mother is warned repeatedly by her sister, the aunt, not to let the intruder take precedence in the household. He has heard the clarity of the one-sided telephone calls, the conversations during which the children's mother, in a voice ringing with reassurance, argues with her sister that it is quite safe, perfectly safe, Darling, to leave this homeless man with the children.

'He only comes once a week, Darling, and if he sleeps over he has the folding bed in the ferns and he's only here for one meal. Yes, Darling, he can have a bath, that's part of the agreement. But only one bath a week ... Alexis? Oh, *you know Alexis*. He's a slave to beauty and our DP has the most soft, melting eyes, dark eyes, long dark lashes and a pale – an *interesting* – complexion. His hands are slender with long fingers. Alexis says, subtle fingers, no Darling not supple, *subtle*, there is a difference. And, the children say that, when he sits in the little cane chair in the conservatory, he most gracefully folds his long legs. Can you imagine!

'Alexis is *waiting* to hear him sing, it was the description we were given of his voice, castrati, yes, a real counter-tenor. But so far our DP hardly speaks a word and then only in a whisper, not a note of anything approaching singing. I mean, for all we know, he might be *bass*. After all, Darling, we must never lose sight of the fact that our Displaced and Homeless person has not come back to the community from his own choice. How shall I put it? He has been *returned*.'

'Don't take any notice,' Ursula has whispered more than once during visits. 'It's just mother and aunty, they've always chewed things over like this. The phone is their life-line. They'll never change. Father says it's expensive but better than having aunty here.'

The house for a Consul and his family is a house for people who, having to move from one country to another, have to become accustomed to change. The house, as it is, offers stability in the heavy furniture, the yards of chintz and the left-over library. It is a house familiar and unfamiliar. Familiar in memories of the untrustworthy kind and unfamiliar in Dalton's own small confidence. He remembers how, as a boy, he longed to be somewhere else, he longed to escape from the glazed material, the bunchings of floral cloth from ceiling to floor, disliked by his mother and aunt Dalton. For them it was a matter of having to accept the choice of the wife of an earlier Consul, as if she excelled with perfect taste, whereas the wife of the representative in trade was expected to have no taste at all.

During the day, sunlight or the grey mists of rain do not alter the dust and the shabbiness of the old house — withering for want of a permanent owner; someone who would cherish the possession of the bricks and the walls, the doors and the windows, the roof beams and those hidden joists supporting, in secret, the floorboards.

The comfort and seclusion of drawn curtains, large armchairs and the hearth are the same as when Dalton, as a boy, felt both safe and trapped. He has not said to any one person in the family that he is familiar with their house, that he lived there once, years ago. And, because of not saying so, the moment for revealing this has gone by. He knows that had he been a different sort of person he could have regaled the family with all kinds of recollections.

Aunt Dalton, one evening, asked his mother if she remembered the name of a singer, a contralto, such a voice with deep notes which reached into the whole body of the listener. Her admirers, she said, trying to bring the name of the singer to mind, brought jewels and threw them down the aisles of the concert hall but she, the well-bred creature, paid not the slightest attention and went on singing as if nothing had happened, and later her maid, a sort of little house-maid, came with her dustpan and brush and swept up all the pearls and rubies. Such homage, aunt Dalton sighed. Neither she nor Dalton's mother could remember the name of the singer.

Dalton has to remind himself that these well-meaning people in the house are completely unlike either aunt Dalton or his mother, and, of course, are unlike himself. He understands that he comes to the house because he has no other choice. Aunt Dalton, if she could know, would laugh and say he was surrounding himself with acres of boredom. His acceptance of his experience causes him to be meek and silent and he is unable to speak to them with the confidence of his education and the gift of his singing voice. There is no need for him to overhear the references in the one-sided telephone conversations to know that he is, for them, forever the unpaying guest, or the DP, the displaced person.

During the uneasy moments on the verandah he thinks of the kitchen which has been completely renovated. He understands enough to know that even if the kitchen is perfect with a welcoming efficiency, warm and bright with coloured bottles and jugs, bulging with the reds and greens and yellows of fresh vegetables and gleaming with the translucent blue and white china — if all these do not hold a special meaning, it is because the kitchen is not inhabited by the wished for people. In this event it is better not to be there, however cold or hungry or lonely he might be. Unless the house holds the laughter of his mother and aunt Dalton and even the voice of his father, it is simply a hollow place and uninviting.

Over the years he has learned that it is wise to flatter people. It is a way of protecting himself. At the same time he has been appalled to see his few false words taking effect. It is clear to him that Cornelius is skilled in this art, perhaps for different reasons, since he seems to take pleasure in seeing the results.

With relief that his timid pressure on the doorbell has not been noticed, he turns and makes for the gate walking away with light steps in the shadow of the hedge.

Now, treading on twigs and memory, he pauses and listens. He is not sure if he hears the faint shuffling of feet following. All is silent and he walks on relieved that he has had the good sense to step off the verandah before he could be discovered there.

It is easy for him to recall that, without actually throwing anything at the Horsefly, years ago in that house, the two women, his mother and his aunt between them, were able to cause his father to raise his arms and his hands making all the movements necessary for protecting his own defenceless head.

Dalton pauses once more, standing very still and close into the hedge. This time he is certain he is being followed. Someone is shuffling through the dry leaves. He catches on the night air the penetrating scent of a powerful antiseptic soap. He thinks it is the soap, the remedy demanded by Winch's skin disease, a wretched symptom in his progressing illness. Distasteful thoughts follow mixed with fear of his fellow lodgers and their patience and their curiosity. There is something sinister in their patience. Now this evening, the soap adds another depth to his uneasiness.

He stands listening. There is no shuffling on the pavement behind him and even the smell of the soap, intense as it was, has disappeared.

At Mrs Porter's, whenever Dalton leaves his room or returns to it, Winch and Perce are either on the stairs or on the landing or in the doorway of their own room. Often they are sharing the bathroom. They seem to be very much in evidence whenever Dalton Foster is coming in or going out. As a rule, one will make a remark to the other, and both will have something to say to Dalton.

Dalton, once again, tells himself that he has imagined that he is being followed.

Headline:	ACCIDENTS FLAWED POLICE
comment:	Mrs Porter:
Mrs Porter:	There's a accident in every cup. You should just see yours EV ... Accidents: Road: Home: Street: Office: Burnings: Drownings: Shootings: Poisonings; you name it, it's done. Street fights, it's all in the tea cup. EV. A loving weekend in the country is coming your way. For eligible only. Menu. Fish and Chips fetched in Tinned peas Bread and Butter Tea and Bingo
Miss Vales:	I never ever clap eyes on him.
Mrs Porter:	Well, he's around all right, EV, coming and going all day he is – up and down the stairs – in and out all the whole day long and half the night ...
Miss Vales:	It's the baby-sitting. I never get the chance ...
Mrs Porter:	Don't be silly, EV, it's the baby-sitting as makes you interesting.

As he walks, Dalton contemplates the beauty of the night. His thoughts dwell on the inner nourishment from his earlier reading and he feels an unexpected sense of harmony between himself and the park. He feels excited to be heightened in this way and resolves to unpack, to *really unpack* his books and papers, his writing, from the unopened tin box which is still standing up-ended, as it was when delivered there, in his room at Mrs Porter's. His elation seems to have come about with the sense of freedom which accompanied the swift walking away from the house before anyone in the house realised he was at the door. It is even more than freedom, it is escape. He does not question this further as he hurries across the soft slopes of the park. In the darkness the grass is intensely fragrant as if crushed from a recent mowing.

'Bearing the burden of your exquisite gifts?' aunt Dalton said to him when she came upon him writing in the summer-house. 'Can you sing what you have written?' she asked him. She picked up a pencil and corrected, delicately, a note. 'A semitone I think here,' she said, 'and you will bring tears to the eyes of all who listen to this.'

It was during the next few days, at that time, that Dalton, reading about the lives of the great composers, began to understand how aspects of human life and feeling could be presented, through all kinds of art, to all kinds of people. He loved words and phrases and he knew, then, that he would devote himself to writing however arduous and unrewarding it might be. During his last year at school he looked forward to being at the university. He was impatient for the life he expected there. He wanted to study and to read and to travel and ultimately to write.

'I'm afraid I have prevented our little wretch from being a genius,' aunt Dalton confessed to his mother later that evening. 'I made one humble correction, in the summer-house, and he has torn up the entire sheet. All the same,' aunt Dalton went on, 'he will attract *sympathy* and, in that way, will become famous, perhaps *notorious* is a better word for his personal destiny. The child's intellectual ability is something which needs, what do the Germans call it, *Durchhaltern*, endurance ... only the Germans would, or could, have a word with a double h in the middle of it,' aunt Dalton said.

❧

All at once, Dalton is sure that he can see the child, ahead of him, moving away with dancing steps. Lifting her feet and pointing her toes, she disappears in a pool of darkness beneath one of the old trees only to appear far off, as if she has flown, and is resting, teasing him, in the faded light of one of the park lamps. Dalton can see and recognise her small ragged dress and her dark hair which, in the lamp light, seems to be decorated with petals. The little girl makes for the black shape of the only building in the park, an ugly brick building, close to the road. Dalton follows her. He will keep her in sight and follow her whichever way she goes. He fondles the apples in his raincoat pocket and is confident that this time he will not lose sight of her.

The park is apparently deserted and Dalton crosses the last slopes with careless leaping strides. Unable to see clearly he falls headlong over the body of a man lying in the grass on the unlit side of the building. He gets up at once, gasping for breath, and stands crouching. The man remains lying with his head resting face down in his folded arms. Dalton starts to speak, to offer an apology.

'Hallo, Sweetheart,' the man rolls over, half sitting up. 'What's your choice? Oil or talc?' His voice is smooth. 'Pick your choice ...' The voice purrs as if carrying a smile inside it.

The child must have gone on down towards the river. If she had gone to the station she would still be visible passing from one street lamp to the next.

Shaken by the sinister encounter, Dalton feels his heart thumping. He tries to believe that he can still see the child. He hurries in the direction he imagines she is going. He turns his thoughts, as he often does in the face of disappointment, to Miss Mallow. He understands, as he hurries downhill, that he has given Miss Mallow and the friend he has created for her, instead of this river, an English river for the proposed outing, the journey on a river boat. A silent river where it is certain to be raining, where silent men sit hunched under waterproof capes fishing in dismal surroundings, overhung with dripping trees and, where the grassy banks break down in places, slippery with mud. He tells himself, his breathing and his steps quickening, that this does not matter since he has never spoken to Miss Mallow about the proposed friend and the treasures of the imagined relationship.

The river, he is approaching, is wide and gleaming like a great lake, light in the night when everything else is dark. Two loose arms of the river spread round a ragged island and two bridges, one immediately after the other, their arches as if following each other and never catching up, are harnessed inevitably by the main road with several lanes of traffic crossing in both directions. The water spanned by this length of bridging is smooth and unemotional on both sides.

The child is ahead of him, now in the lights of passing cars, now hidden in shadow. Suddenly she disappears as if she has fallen from the narrow footpath on the second bridge. Dalton, catching up, determined on his prey, quickens his step and slides after her straight down the remnants of broken steps, a steep path of mud and broken bricks and is, all at once, on the flat earth of the bank beneath the bridge. The water, black under the bridge, laps with a faint sighing along the mid-river structure. Above, the cars and buses pass with varying sound and vibration. To the left a small damp fire is smouldering at the water's edge. One or two people are bending over and moving about, hovering perhaps, in this inadequate firelight. All at once, from above and behind him, there is an angry exchange of words, a noise reminiscent of the parrots quarrelling over their roosting places. Women's voices, an old hoarse voice and another voice, young, perhaps a girl but not the little girl, his little girl. She is always silent. The voices are raised in a desperation of anger. Dalton moves closer to the iron and concrete pillar at the side of the narrow shaft, the precipitous way, down which he had followed the child. He feels his heart beating, thumping in his chest and all over his body, the beating is especially noticeable in his head.

'It's Doreen's bedplace.' He hears the shrill cry. 'It's Doreen's bedplace.' Across on the other side of the small fire his own chosen little girl is sobbing. She darts forward over the fire and pulls at the clothing of a big girl who, in the poor light, could be an older girl or a woman. Dalton can see that she is solidly built with thick bare thighs which glisten with the scales of a rash angry and visible in the sudden leap of flame in the fire. Her coarse hair is long and tangled and hides her face. She is struggling and fighting with someone. Within the double eyesight of the two bridges something terrible is happening. Dalton, an unwilling yet compelled audience, moves closer.

An old woman is lodged as if stuck, having forced herself backwards into a sort of earthen shelf between the steep bank and the next concrete pillar. As the traffic passes overhead, the bank of earth, making the roof of the shelf, trembles and seems to move slightly, pressing downwards. In the half-choked screams and words between the girl and the old woman, Dalton understands that the old woman was the first there that night and has taken over the dirt ledge which, in a succession of screams, the big girl says is hers, by rights.

Dalton, unable to do anything, watches the fight which is accompanied by more screaming and which ends with the old woman being dragged by her hair and her rags of clothing with such violence that, all at once, she is lying bleeding, naked and deformed with injury, at the soft edges of the river. The girl sobs, scarcely able to draw breath; she seems to be calling the woman by some name. It sounds almost like an endearment. Crying still she kneels down over the body in a magnificence of remorse. Her crying is softer and she seems to be talking in a low and loving voice to the lifeless body.

Suddenly she stops crying and, getting up, she stands staring at the corpse. There is a silence, a silence smelling of mud and river water. It is a sudden silence, to Dalton, a dreadful silence of terror and secret awe. A silence which seems to be shrouding the regular sounds of the traffic passing both ways overhead. He supposes that this silence must accompany all disaster especially murder. It is suddenly very cold. This sudden cold and the blackness, these are also a part of murder. And then there is fear. A previously unthought of fear. A silent fear which holds the heart and the mind, preventing thought and movement, preventing speech, catching the breath causing an inability to breathe, and a closing of the throat, a sensation of choking.

For the first few minutes Dalton is not able to see the little girl. He sees instead that there are many more people in this place. They gather round with stealth, silent and menacing, sliding from the higher-up places on the steep parts of the bank and from behind the third and fourth concrete pillars. There is the crackling sound of a small radio, and a talkback-show host, as if with a clothes peg on his nose, is announcing in a calm voice that Steve is surprisingly consulted by one of the gardeners about her lack of orgasm and will Mrs Bellows come to the telephone as she has just been announced as the winner of a double pass for dinner at the Grand Hotel. 'Mrs Bellows, you have ...'

'Turn that shit off,' a voice growls in the darkness. A heavy boot kicks the remains of the fire apart. Without another word and, as if with common consent, the body is pushed and rolled into the river. It is a silent, slow-moving communal act finished off by one of them, wading up to his neck, as far as the middle structure of the bridge, guiding the floating corpse out, past this point, where, Dalton notices for the first time, there is some movement of current. The water seems sluggishly powerful there. In silence the others watch as the body floats and then sinks out of sight. The rags of clothing are taken out next and left to follow their owner. The smell of the river water and the disturbed mud seems suddenly stronger as if heralding further action.

Almost at once, as if his presence has been sensed by some sinister instinct or power of perception, the little group, once more as if with a communal consent, turn and move slowly towards him. Dalton hears the child crying close by.

'Doreen, it's your bedplace. It is, Doreen,' he hears the frightened little voice.

'Shaddap!' a man's voice growls.

'Are you looking for someone?' another voice behind Dalton speaks. 'Is it a little talk you're wanting? Is it time we had a little talk, you and me?' Dalton recognises the voice of the man in the park, the owner of the choice offered earlier in the park. He understands, at once, that he is trapped between these people, the concrete pillar and the black water. He understands too, for the first time, that the little girl was never alone in the park as he thought. He puts his hand in his pocket and feels the apples.

'No, you don't,' the man is very close, standing over him so that escape is not possible.

As he falls Dalton is certain that there are no eyes for this. These people will not see any of it. He feels the intense pain as he is punched and kicked. Someone sits on his chest and presses his neck. He sinks into the mud. His unprotesting body is pushed and rolled to the edge of the water. He feels the cold water soak into his clothes. He is surrounded by silence which holds only the sighing of the river. He remembers reading something once about the arches of two bridges being like eyes looking at each other but unable to speak.

'*C'est le tombeau des secrets.*' Aunt Dalton's useful little phrase refuses to be formed in his swollen and mud-filled mouth. I won't tell anyone anything, he promises somewhere inside his head. He is not sure if he has been lying beneath the expressive but silent arches of the bridges for days or hours or simply for a few minutes. He tries to raise his head. His body is numb and heavy, cold in the wet clothes. There was a nursery rhyme years ago. He tries to remember the words; *something, something, my son John went to bed with his stockings on.* No, that was not right, the rhythm is all wrong. *Poor Jim Jay got stuck fast in yesterday.* That was closer to the truth but was not the rhyme he was trying to remember. It was all nonsense. He wanted to sleep and to wake up from the dream. To sleep alongside a nursery rhyme was nice but he had to move on from coloured crayons to the refined enchantment of the Christmas painting box. The names of the colours, to begin with, were mysterious; ultra-marine, Prussian blue, cobalt blue, then there was orange and then green and yellow, brown and purple like the river after heavy rain. The black and white were in fat little tubes. Then there was the yellow ochre, the burnt sienna and all the different reds, vermilion, crimson lake, rose, rose madder — Rose! He calls to Rose to come, remembering that Rose is always far too busy. But there is aunt Dalton instead, loving the colours, wanting him to wet the paint brush in the little glass of clear water she holds out to him.

'Try the yellow ochre,' she says. She loves the yellow ochre. 'Try it wet,' she pleads. Dalton wants to drink the water. The colour is dirty, he dislikes the colour. He is crying, wanting water. The yellow colour is for rags. He asks for clean water. Aunt Dalton, like Rose, has gone ...

'Dirty work. Don't cry. No need to cry.' Voices? He is always hearing their voices. Perce and Winch, they talk all the time. He hears their nonchalant conversations from the doorway of the bathroom. There, in that place, they are the perfection of harmony and friendship. The one yields his place in the bathroom to the other. Their cigarette smoke, mingling, curls out across the landing. Both have recently combed their wet hair, slicking it back from the forehead, each in turn using the same comb, holding it under the tap, passing it to and fro. Their voices too pass to and fro, back and forth. They speak to each other with that intimacy of complete understanding, using head and shoulder movements and words which are scarcely articulate. The perfect arrangement, a conversation which is both exclusive and sinister.

※

He is sinking. The mud is giving way and he is going down, down in the softness. Comfortable mud. Unlike himself, Cornelius and Ursula, at the present time, are not able to fit themselves into their surroundings, whereas he is perfectly comfortable. They are still in the last place where their father had an appointment. They are still, in their hearts, making a musical and artistic pilgrimage in Vienna and hoping to continue this in Dresden shortly. To be in Australia is very much removed from their thoughts and the kind of life they desire. The presence of Monsieur Perdu assists in the creation of the fairytale world of hunting lodge and passion. It is true that their mother clearly loves her homeland and knows how to thrive in it. But even she relishes the tutor. For her, he is both a dancing master and an exotic acquisition. He provides the opportunity for the hesitant French in single words delivered with laughter and stammering. It is a kind of broken English and a shattered French, accompanied with elaborate movements of the hands and the shoulders. The eyes become part of the speech with quick glances and a vivacious appearance of intelligence. The English words are often spoken with accents which are foreign but not necessarily French.

Dresden and Vienna had not required Dalton, T for Trade, Foster for more than two weeks respectively. Dalton recalls easily the heart-broken cries from his mother and aunt Dalton when they had to make do with an industrial town on the Rhine where there was some interest in brushes and reels of cotton thread made in Britain. It was clear once more that the insignificant Horsefly should have been standing behind the counter in an ironmonger's shop selling wooden cooking spoons and counting nails and screws.

Mercifully the kicking and punching is over. He has not been beaten to death. The people have gone and it is very quiet with only the sounds of the water at the edge of the mud and the intermittent traffic passing overhead. Sometimes the passing cars hold a rhythm as of a train crossing points or moving from one line to another with a pleasing sustained regularity of repetition. This is because the road is made with the surface ridged at intervals, something perhaps necessary for the con-struction of the bridges. As the sounds of one imagined train fade, other sounds, from the other direction, continue the illusion.

One time when they were travelling, his mother and aunt Dalton took him, by train, to Zürich. Between

Geneva and Lausanne a waiter, in uniform, with a small trolley, came through the train asking the passengers, in French, if they wanted something to eat. And then between Lausanne and Berne the same man came through again with his trolley, this time asking everyone in German if they wanted coffee. Aunt Dalton enjoyed, she said, the luxury of the fragrant coffee, the warm croissants and the honey, which made little golden pools on their plate, while the neat fields and the winding roads of the countryside slipped by in the soothing rocking of the express train.

Dalton remembers now that Lake Geneva is surrounded by hills, the foothills of the Swiss and the French Alps. And almost all the hills have pretty villages perched on them and the lower slopes are ribbed and decorated with vineyards.

Though unable to move, Dalton's thoughts are changing fast. He can explain, if given the chance, that one thought is following the previous thought with scarcely a pause. He is sure the hours are passing quickly and the hours are filled with thoughts.

Aunt Dalton, he remembers, said that the Swiss made rather soft benign wines. And his mother reminded aunt Dalton that the bookshops in Lausanne were excellent. Aunt Dalton, he gives a small sigh, persuaded him, as always, to eat.

When he was the same age as either Ursula or Cornelius he was unable to adapt to change. Aunt Dalton always said so. She made an announcement of it. He should really explain this to the two children. He was never able, in the much used phrase, to accept his place in society, he will tell them, since he never knew what it was.

His life, it seemed then, depended on his father's eagerness for the next place. But this hope that the next place would be better than anything ever experienced was always accompanied by the sulky frowns and cross words from his mother and aunt Dalton. As time went by the reality of the dreariness became more unbearable, they said, for them. Dalton's mother wept often.

Dalton easily, now, remembers his father's energetic and enthusiastic way of walking and describing. He could make an ordinary house brick, a 'red-brick' brick seem like a wonderful invention, a magical ingredient for the building of special houses and castles.

'Is mother in?' his father asked him during the special visit. His father's pale eyes seemed very close to him where he sat near the pillow. His father's eyes filled with tears which were not allowed to overflow.

'Is your mother in?' his father often spoke using the possessive 'your'. 'Where's your anti Dalton?' he would say. Dalton had to remind him that his mother had died some years ago; 'Don't you remember?' he asked his father, noticing an indignation in his own voice, an attempt to hide the trembling weakness of the sounds in his own throat. 'Mother died,' he said, regretting the brutality.

His father said then that he wanted to come home. More than anything he wanted to be at home. Couldn't Dalton take him home there and then? Surely he could. He remembered their home, he said, and he wanted to be back there. When he tried to describe the place where he wanted to be, Dalton knew which place it was, but was afraid to help his father to the pain of remembering completely. The nurses, they sent Dalton away while they washed his father. He was dressed in a white gown drawn up by tapes at the neck and the wrists.

In the pictures in his mind, in his imagination, his father told him there was always a place of grass and blossom and trees. Not noticing that Dalton was trying to take a surreptitious glance at his watch, he went on to say that he had lost his way, long ago, in the seasons and had let them run together, the sweet flowers of narcissus in small bunches and the almond blossom bursting out along the thin branches before the leaves. Did Dalton remember, he wanted to know, that the almond blossom would open in the house if you put the twigs in a jar of clean water? It was like his father to say clean water instead of just water. And then there would be the honeysuckle: he described the flowers nestling in the shiny green leaves and reminded Dalton about the doves. Did Dalton remember the doves, he wanted to know, the doves, he said, round breasted, pink and tawny in the last light of the fast disappearing sun. Though these birds are fierce, his father persisted, his voice strong, *fierce*, he said, in dispossessing other birds — there is *nothing* in a man's life, in his freedom, to challenge his own determination, early in the evening to choose whether to walk or to go to bed. Why couldn't he, his fingers pulling at the sheet, why, he wanted to know, was he not able to walk in the evening? It was getting dark quickly he reminded Dalton. Recollecting, he explained briefly a frequent irritation. The demented inmate, in the next bed repeatedly, from his bed, leaned across and with a kind of mindless and systematic destructive movement removed Dalton's father's blanket. The ensuing rage provoked violence for which, his father said, the victim (himself) could be placed in isolation.

Knowing that his visit to his father's bedside was allowed for compassionate reasons, he expected that the special bus would be waiting for him. His father, quiet after his brief anger about the blanket, began to speak again just as Dalton was sliding with bent legs from his chair. He listened to his father and allowed himself to recapture something of the old magic as his father, in a low voice, began to talk about the time when the water rose, after heavy rain, and flooded with soft sounds over the boards of a little wooden bridge. As he strained to hear his father's voice it was as if he had beside him, all over again, like a special present, the indulgent playfellow of his childhood, entirely uncritical and patient and offering always unconditional love and consolation, his father ...

Dalton recalls now, as this memory fades, all too easily, his father small and pinched looking in the hospital bed, smaller than on the previous visit. He remembers the thin ineffectual fingers moving up in an attempt to push away the oxygen mask during the struggle for more air. There seemed to be no one about. The oxygen cylinder, he remembers unwillingly, seemed to him to be empty. He wants, with the helpless wanting when it is too late, to have been a help to his father at that time.

'Father?' He hears his own voice; 'Father?' an unfamiliar word on his lips. There was that time when his own voice, the voice of the little boy, frightened, called to his father when the father, caught in the strong currents of the Danube, almost drowned. A man fishing from a small boat, obviously regarding the waving arm as a greeting, simply concentrated on his fishing. His father did not drown but saved himself as he was carried by the swift river (he always laughed, later on, whenever he related the adventure), close enough to a small wooden jetty ...

It was an illness which ended what seemed to the child, and later the adult, to be a whole lifetime, wherein a deeply felt realisation of a painful and lasting failure in marriage could not be healed. Not even the tiny drops of secret pleasure and excitement in moments of a modest success in his work could soothe his disappointment. Nothing could compensate for the sense of the unsuccessful which had to be kept hidden. It was both a suffering and a sorrow which remained in the heart, unspoken, and was only ever minutely revealed, occasionally, by a small unguarded look or gesture.

So vivid was the telling about the man, the demented one, pulling and working at the blanket and removing it from the other patient (his father), that Dalton felt, at the time, that the experience had been his own. Certainly the exasperation which brings about, at times, his sense of isolation is his own and not simply his father's ...

ॐ

The bedside scene, which returns often, fades when Dalton considers the possibility that the park, in darkness, will be deserted. There will be no one of the troublesome or unpleasant sort there. The child, though, is almost certain to be there. He has never, he realises, been through the park without seeing her. He sees her always in snatches, in tiny glimpses, ahead of him as a small delicate painting in subdued colours. He suspects that her little clothes are merely rags. The park, the enchanted place of grass and flowers, belongs now to his father. He claimed the enchantment while he was dying and still able to talk. And then there was the voice which Dalton recognised as the voice of silence which had persisted during the years and which, in the last breathing, cried out in heart-breaking despair. Recalling this voice, this cry which has, all through the years, lingered in his hearing, Dalton remembers his father's wise and gentle ways and he wants to speak to his father and to tell him the things he never did say to him.

'Father! I want to tell you, I ... Father?'

❧

'You farver ain't here, matey.'

'Take a look, willya. Look at that. They've left him for dead.'

'That's right. That's what they've done.'

'They've busted his jaw. You reckon?'

'And his ribs. I'll lay a bet on that.'

'They've spread his nose all over his face. Take a look there.'

'Unbelievable!'

'That's what they've done. He's all over blood.'

There are voices above going to and fro, near and then far away. Two voices, to and fro, back and forth.

'Can you move Mr Foster?' Someone bends down close. 'Mr Foster, can you move at all?'

'We was right behind you, Mr Foster, can you move? Can you get up?'

Someone is shining a small flashlight in his eyes. The other man strikes a match.

'I saw them,' Dalton tries to speak. 'I saw them murder ...' His lips are painful and thick. His head seems to reverberate with pain. 'I saw them murder the old woman.'

'You, *you saw nothink*. Remember that.'

'That's right. You was just out for a walk – '

'An' you slepped in the mud. You wasn't here you didn't slep here. Savvy? You was somewhere else.'

'Excepting, but, Perce they seen him. There's the trouble. He'll have to lay low.'

'It's us, Mr Foster. It's the both of us. It's us two,

Perce and Wench here, Mr Foster. We're going to get you home somehow. A good theng we follered Mr Foster, eh? Wench?'

'You can say that again, Perce.'

✗

'What was you going to do with the penk ladies?' Perce wanted to know suddenly in the silence. 'The penk ladies what had you in mind?"'

'Pink ladies?' Dalton had difficulty with the words.

'Yes, these.' The three apples, as the two tired men propped up the third on the bridge, caught the moonlight and were, for a moment, silver. Three silver apples of the moon resting on a dirty outstretched hand.

Aunt Dalton, whenever they were near the railway, declared her love for the trains, especially the long freight trains in Australia. The sound of a wheat train passing during the night recalls for Dalton the half-heard conversations when his mother and aunt Dalton, returning, crept into the hotel bedroom where he had been put to bed earlier. The wheat train, the heavy engines, two of them, the rumbling of the wagons following and the long drawn-out melodious horn did have, as aunt Dalton said, something in common with the singing voice. Don Giovanni, for example, she insisted. Both contained, she said, in their drum roll and in their timbre the musical sound, the pitch, the intensity, all the delight and the burden of a mounting expectation and passion, the burden being, in particular, because of the urgent need for release. Often, on returning from the opera, aunt Dalton would declare that unless the special dramatic and emotional qualities, within the heart and desire of the composer, are given to the voice and the accompanying instruments, the tone and the cadence, the hardly perceptible, the *elusive* slipping from one key to another, so essential to the art, is lost.

Aunt Dalton and his mother would creep about the room, taking off each other's fine dresses and brushing each other's hair, all the time speaking in hushed whispers in order that Dalton, supposedly asleep in his little bed in a corner of the room, would not be disturbed.

They agreed, their hoarse voices cracking, as always, that it was not a simple mixture of powerful orchestration and voices enriched by plates of rare beef which could make a present-day opera (perhaps written from a contemporary novel) achieve the same emotional heights which, they both, in turn, insisted could only spring from the heart and from the most noble and deeply felt desire.

'The power of restraint, Darling,' aunt Dalton would say, 'the tenor has, the whole time he's on stage, to be restraining his unbridled passion.'

Aunt Dalton often sang in her bath after these conversations. 'After all,' she confided in Dalton's mother, 'it's the same with the soprano and the contralto – you agree?' Dalton imagined them both in the bath, their long hair floating.

Breathing in his mother's perfume, he slept.

❧

'In the morning, when you've had a rest,' Perce is saying somewhere in the room, 'we'll show you somethink special, somethink trooly beautiful, won't we, Wench.'

'Too right,' Winch says, bending closer to his work. Dalton can feel the warm wet cloth Winch is applying to his painful face.

'Bring us a drop more hot water, Perce.' Winch straightens up and then bends forward once more, wiping the wet cloth in small circles over the pain.

'Don't talk,' he tells Dalton. He tells him to hush up as they are now within range of connubial missiles. Perce explains that Winch has learned these words at night school and wants to use them. He stands to one side of Winch with a fresh bowl of hot water.

'You're going to have to lay low,' Perce says. 'Wench an' me we'll get stuff for you from the chemist. We don't thenk you've broke any bones, isn't that so, Wench?'

'Quite right, Perce. His nose has took some alteration, but. Easy now! Don't you try getting off that bed, Mr Foster.' Perce takes the cloth from Winch. 'Lie back down, Mr Foster.'

Dalton, through his half-closed swollen eyelids, is able to see he is in his own room and on his own bed. He tries to speak, to ask questions.

'We was in luck all right,' Perce explains. 'We saw you beat up and *they* never seen us. And then on the bridge, that taxi, remember? He threw out a coupla drunks. Said he didn't want no chunder. Blood, he said, all right, and mud all right ... And Mr Foster, I know it's not for me to say this but you done something very foolish and dangerous. We, Wench and me, was afraid you would try to do summat. You can't take anybody and look after them yourself. I don't like to be the one to have to say this but you can't even invite a little girl or a boy in to tea, even if you've got tenned frewt and sardines, because you're not in the level of people who can do this. And it's no use you sleeping out as a protest. You'll just be told to move on or else you'll be picked up. Get this straight, it's for *ladies* to do this money raising for schools and clothes and they raise what they call public awareness. So it's not for you, Mr Foster. I hope you'll excuse me.'

Dalton feels he ought to explain his selfish motives and that he simply wanted the little girl ... 'I must tell ...' he tries to speak.

'Wench here,' Perce interrupts and hands back the cloth to Winch. 'Wench here, was sure you was done for. Isn't that right, Wench?' He pauses. 'Don't ask how we got you up them stairs and not a soul about to ask us what we was doing. Isn't that right, Wench?'

'*The need for scholarship and study,*' Winch seems to be reciting, '*to understand the ideal perfection that is only rarely expressed in the work itself ...*'

'Ain't that just grand!' Perce says. 'Wench here gets all that from night school. The only trouble is they don't tell him what he can do with it.'

Dalton, feeling the blankets being put over him and patted into place over his feet, is reminded of the times, in different hotels, when he was a child, lying on different sofas, crying and laughing. On one of these occasions aunt Dalton patted soft travelling rugs all over him, squeezing his feet in an affectionate way, telling him that, if he slept, there would be a surprise for him later, something beautiful. Trying to sleep then, he closed his eyes. Aunt Dalton, crooning softly to him, simultaneously talked to his mother, saying that she hoped, no, *yearned* was a better word, to see the physical thrill of the pure love-sick tenor or, better still, the perfection of two or more voices in harmony, a duet or perhaps a quartet, pass through the little wretch's body. Dalton knew then, overhearing the whispered conversation, that he had already felt aunt Dalton's wish for him, but secretly, with the soprano and the contralto in orphean excellence and, carefully, had sheltered this within his private experience.

Being settled now on the pillow and covered with the blanket reminds Dalton of the toy theatre which aunt Dalton unpacked during that particular illness. There was a miraculous perfection about the little theatre. It had a proscenium arch, decorated with velvet folds of crimson and gold, revealing partly naked women, with voluptuous thighs and bosoms, entwined with vine leaves and rosebuds. This arch framed a neat little wooden stage which had two trap doors and several different backdrops for scenes; a ship's captain's cabin, a ballroom, a hide-out for thieves, a cave filled with jewels, a castle for kings and queens and a magic forest in which trees walked and animals were able to speak. It was possible then to create all kinds of stories of human conflict, violence, danger, thought and resolution. Even his present condition, this scene of pain, could have been placed then, at this little distance of 'Let's pretend', as it begins to fade in the comfort of warm clean water and the gentle towel and now the welcome blankets.

'You can if you like,' Dalton told his father who came for a few minutes to sit on the sofa; 'you can if you like, throw a sailor overboard or put him under the floorboards or see, this one can walk the plank, *it's a theatre.*'

'Yes,' his father said, 'you can make some good tales.' He was enthusiastic. 'And remember,' he said, 'a good story, a fiction as they call it, has to have something comforting happen at intervals — during the adversity, the audience will want to see justice and achievement, that's what people like to see. Adversity,' his father went on, 'that's a hard word, shall I spell it for you and explain its meaning?'

'I can spell it,' Dalton said, 'and I know what it means.'

❧

'He'd better have a bath come the morning,' the voice interrupts. It is Winch. 'I'm saying, Mr Foster, to Perce, here, that you'll enjoy having a bath in the morning.' The short 'a' in Winch's pronounciation of bath recalls, for Dalton, immediately his father's voice, his sharp nose and the keen expression in his eyes when he was describing a place, a view and especially when he was describing a particular product, perhaps at a trade dinner evening; a lengthy ceremonial meal, seen through the open doors at the end of the hotel ballroom, all in black and white, the black dinner jackets, the white shirts and the black bow ties with the two women providing the only splashes of colour, pink with cream lace (Dalton's mother) and aunt Dalton striking in an emerald-green sheath.

'Like an officer's boot, my dear,' Dalton's mother screamed while they were dressing. 'Like an officer's thigh boot,' her voice intense with the pleasure of aunt Dalton's exquisite elegance resembling the handsome booted leg of a cossack, she said then, 'descending with virile intentions from his horse.'

174

Dalton's father was anxious to please the guests and to promote aspects of trade between the countries represented at the awesome tables. Dalton, lingering near the open double doors, surveyed the party and heard his father's eager voice.

'Then there's the Orange Pekoe, there's a beautiful tea, a fine leaf tea, delicate and sweet natured yet strong enough to make a good brew. The Earl Grey too, that's a bigger leaf but not inferior for all that, not a bit of it. I'll tell you, gentlemen, what makes a fragrant beverage, you put two measures of Earl Grey and one of Orange Pekoe. Gentlemen! I will draw attention to these little silvery scoops here, a whole set of them, every one with an English castle for a handle. Well, two scoops of the Earl Grey and one of the Orange Pekoe. And, as we all know, the English Castles are very acceptable all over the world ...'

Dalton watching, half hidden in the folding double doors, knew that his mother would cringe from his father's voice and his pronounciation of 'castle'. Aunt Dalton would be shaking with the laughter contained within her brilliant carapace. This hidden laughter about to burst from its shell caused the two women to rise from the table and, excusing themselves, make for the double doors. 'Oh that Horsefly! Just listen to him. The Excruciating Bore!'

His father's head was large and well shaped. If in the early days at Cambridge there had been excited discussion about a head, his father's head, it would have been described as noble and classical. Someone would have compared the head with the famous sculpture saying it was stern and aesthetic, resembling the bronze head of Voltaire.

In spite of his fine head he was shy and respectful. Because of this he walked with his shoulders bent and rounded and, at the same time, he held his head up, thrown back, as if to increase his height and to catch the fresh unbreathed air. And, in spite of his father's position in relation to the dinner-table guests, it seemed to Dalton then, that in the presence of his wife and his sister, his father was, if not really a horsefly (for how could a human being be an insect?), nothing more than a small insignificant bird with its bedraggled breast feathers puffed up, ragged, and its head lifted up, singing with an inadequate voice while perched, helpless, in the swaying branches of a dying cypress.

There seemed to be no intervals in his father's life, no times of emotional and spiritual refreshment and renewal. His life was an immense tragedy in one devastating act on a set stage which could not be changed and replaced with other scenes. Unlike his own experience, all this was far too great and far too deep and large to place in the simple middle distance of make believe in the clean prettiness of the tiny stage of the toy theatre.

The melancholy horn, distant at first, and then approaching the level crossing, close to Mrs Porter's place, and then the sustained rumbling of the wagons passing on the other side of the cyclone fence, rolling over the points one after the other, going on to fade into that miraculous meeting of land and sea where the grain ships, docked in safe harbour, wait for the arrival of their cargo, all this reminds Dalton that, though facing the engine was considered to be desirable for travelling and essential for his mother and aunt, sitting with his back, he discovered, to the engine in the long transcontinental trains was far better. Looking back, along the way they had just come, and seeing the fields and the farms and the forests slipping by, one scene after another, had a magical effect which, in every way, exceeded the need to place the body biologically facing in the direction in which the train was travelling. In the backward glance, tree trunks rose out of the mist on the almost perpendicular slopes of a ravine, a bridge, just crossed, could be seen to have three arches, and, because of long winding curves, there were touching glimpses of the final carriages swaying as they rounded these curves.

⁂

'It'll be shock, Wench,' the voice drifts across Dalton. He tries to open his eyes. Some light from the high-up windows reflects on the ceiling with that pale rosiness which heralds another day. He can see Perce and Winch, very close to his face, peering at him.

'It'll be shock, Wench,' Perce says. 'Mr Foster's in shock, that's all. There's bound to be shock after the beatin' he's took. Was you dreaming, Mr Foster? It'll be dreams, that's all. We'll raise your feet, Mr Foster. Wench an' me, we're going to raise your feet.' Perce puts a fat, but gentle, hand on Dalton's head.

'Creep down the back stairs, Wench and find a 'ot water bottle, if you can. Go down quiet. I'll hold up Mr Foster's legs a while.'

'Sure it's not an infection?' Winch drapes the blanket up over the raised legs.

'Go down quiet,' Perce says. 'I've got his legs.'

'My father,' Dalton tells Perce, 'I've never told anyone this. My father used to sell tea, door to door. One lady had three daughters, all married. She bought tea for herself and for the daughters. My father sat in the lady's front room to write out the orders. He delivered the

178

tea, the same week, in the evenings. He walked from the bus or the train carrying two cases packed with tea. It was to get himself into a better position, he was studying then.' The hot tears squeeze from under the swollen lids. Dalton, perplexed, tries to wipe his eyes, but his arms are stiff. Perce lowers Dalton's legs.

'It's orright,' Perce says. His buttons are bursting on his chest. He pulls out a handkerchief and wipes Dalton's face. 'You'll be right,' he says, 'it's shock. That's all it is.'

Dalton, with Perce's hand so close to his face, sees the delicate movement of this hand and the fat fingers which seem clumsy but are not. The movement of the fingers and the outwardly curved arms and the gentle way in which the tears are wiped away cause Dalton to weep more. The arms and the hands seem to move as if in a dance. Dalton sees that Perce is in his uniform, he and Winch must have been sleeping in their clothes as, indeed, he is himself.

'Might as well make a night of it eh? Wench?' Perce holds the cup for Dalton to drink, he puts one thick arm under Dalton's head. 'Hot black with three sugars,' he says.

Dalton wants to know how it is that they have a kettle.

Perce tells him that it is an electric kettle. 'Wench,' he explains, 'put his foot down when Mrs P wanted him to double. Needed more rent money or double, she said. Wench here wouldn't come at it. Wanted perks he told her.'

'She's after the rooms,' Winch explains. 'If she tries the doubling stunt with you, don't have a bar of it till you get what you want.'

The hot steam from the tea is soothing to Dalton's face. He wants to tell them, Perce and Winch, that he is grateful.

'You lay back,' Perce says. 'We'll fix a bath for you early morning and we'll show you, like I said, something trooly beautiful, in the morning.'

The voices fade with the closing of the door and Dalton lies still beneath his blankets. He closes his eyes with the hope of sleep. All at once he is expected to wake up. There is the bright flashing light and the harsh voices shouting to tell the men to get on parade. In a few seconds they are expected to wake and to stand upright in their nakedness beside their beds while the guards make their routine nocturnal examinations. All the men have this same experience, expected and unexpected, during the nights. Whatever compassion they might feel, one for another, it is never expressed. Comfort is never given and is never received.

The group therapy, as he remembers it, takes place in one of the several small rooms. A circle of chairs, the men seated without desks, exposed. There is freshly washed linoleum and the sound of boots sticking on the moist surface. There is the ever-present smell of empty but unwashed ash trays. Except for their clothes, their clothes all being the same, a kind of undress uniform, dark-green trousers loose at the knees and tight at the ankles and matching collarless shirts, they seem to be ordinary men.

They are supposed to talk about themselves and the things they have or have not done. The room is dimly lit. Sometimes the light brightens suddenly, like a small search light, illuminating their faces in turn. The men are supposed to address their remarks to each other by name. Some do this in a self-conscious, half-teasing, half-bullying manner but mostly they speak or mutter as if to the floor. Mainly they describe their boredom and the stupidity of people they know. Their lives are pointless, they say; they describe, as well, how they do not like other people's eyes looking at them. They say they are frightened when other people are frightened of them. All the things they say are in newspaper-reporting phrases. It is as if they have learned to repeat these like a lesson, even the descriptions they give of victims and witnesses are spoken in this way.

The cigarette smoke, they are allowed to smoke at these times, makes his eyes water, or is it because he is, once again, unable to stop weeping from somewhere inside himself? It is all so close in his thoughts ...

❧

Shivering, Dalton is awake once more and allows himself the luxury of gratitude that he is in the quietness of his own room. Once more he must try to sleep. He has discovered, long ago, that ten minutes on the edge of an uneasy sleep is enough to allow a lifetime of experience to return either to haunt or to enrich. There can be no choice between the qualities of enrichment and nightmare. Similarly, what choice is there between people? Which person can be trusted and which one should be avoided? What do his fellow lodgers really want from him, and what about the family at the house? What do they want? From one minute to the next, as he drifts from one troublesome thought to the next, he can be, whether he wants to be or not, in any place or at any time in his life.

Frequently during the slow hours of the night, incidents, images and people present themselves dissolving as quickly as they appear.

Dalton can imagine the Consul's wife and her friends, wrapped in plastic and newspapers, trying to sleep on park benches or in the doorways of hotels and offices. He understands why they are doing this and he understands that their communal shrieks of laughter will help them to endure. As soon as he can, he will explain to Cornelius. A shelf scratched out in the bank under the bridge, like a hole a dog might make for himself, is not a suitable sleeping place for anyone. And certainly such a hole in the dirt does not merit a fight to the death between contenders for this poorest of beds. If he is ever able to walk again, he tells himself, on his next visit to the house, he will explain to Cornelius and to Ursula, naturally keeping the details of the horrible sight of the beaten and drowned corpse to himself. He will emphasise the cold unfriendly night and the inevitable wind and rain, the relentless rain ...

It was raining heavily without any sign of the clouds clearing. Dalton had on his new yellow boots and his matching oilskins. He stood on the wooden bridge as the water rose flowing over the planks and over his boots. His father, slipping on the mud and laughing, had both hands full of paper boats. He set the boats floating and they came towards the bridge swiftly spinning and sinking. Dalton's father said that the last boat was the best and the biggest and the strongest and this was the boat in which his mother and his aunty (he pronounced it anti) would come home from France across the English Channel. Dalton poked at the boat with a stick to bring it to the bank but it, too, was sucked in the flow of the rising water and sank on the other side of the bridge. His father, laughing, said it was, after all, only a game.

❧

The pain persists in one place and then another; lurking in the uncertainty between wakefulness and sleep. Dalton tries to raise his hands to his head but finds the stiffness in his arms prevents this. He wishes he could take off his damp and dirty clothes. He looks forward to the promised bath. He has no way of knowing if Perce and Winch will do all they have promised. He tries to think of a motive for their kind behaviour. Perhaps they want his money. He is ashamed of the thought. A small amount of money is what keeps him a little higher than the destitute. It keeps him forever in a level of dreariness.

The men in the group at the rehabilitation centre repeated, one after the other, the phrases they had learned. These phrases were the confessions which they repeated daily to each other but which might have been said from father to son and from son to father. They were simple explanations, learned by heart, about communication, fear, lack of familiarity, loss of love and unacknowledged contempt. The men were never able to offer explanations other than the standard answers they were encouraged to give. Sitting in their half circle they gazed at the recently washed linoleum. They all, in turn, uttered the same phrases. All, like Dalton himself, had the same things to say. All of them said that they had not been able to talk to or listen to their fathers. The gift of affection was locked up instead of being developed and used. This inborn gift was suffocated in the conventional acceptable behaviour expected within the family and in the community. Affection, the showing and the experience of affection, was feared as a sign of weakness and a forerunner of corruption. Families, single members of whole families, were accused by neighbours. Within the community there seemed to be no place for affection and no time for it. There were improvements to be made to houses, and families looked only towards outward success for their children. There was contentment in living without fresh ideas, simply following events and revelations in newspapers. They lost or never had the ability to admit to real feelings or even to see what feelings were developing in themselves and in their children. Dalton knew, all along, the whole time, that all this could not be pushed into a man's mind. It had to be felt and acknowledged through experience, the search for true affection and the ability to receive affection and, more importantly, to be the giver of affection. Dalton knew that, like himself, the other men held on to the explanations, repeating them but unable to do anything with them. It was like having to hang on to a boat, in rough weather, that single act, for oneself, being all that was possible.

They could know too, from the telling, that the conflict between wish and law was regarded as the crime.

Racists and *homophobics* Greyhead dropping single words disconnected, *widespread* he said, and left the next word suspended in silence till the next day. *Unforgivable* one day, *affectation* the next. *False sentimentality,* a week later. His bulk, blocking the passage or a doorway, his blue-ice eyes, pale, bulging with some hidden exertion. *People,* he said, *contemporary convenience,* his expression unchanging, *on guard,* the words a wealth of conversation in single utterances.

They had to understand, he surprised them, that there was, in society *out there,* an *ever increasing contrast between the rich and the poor. Take it or leave it.* After this he was silent, apart from the occasional warning, a sort of growl from behind his broad leather belt and his bunch of keys, for several days.

An intelligent man, it was clear to Dalton, though he never spoke of this, an intelligent man, if he wanted to be a criminal could, during discussions, become even more cunning in his crimes. He could rise above the prevailing levels of apathetic ignorance and possess a superior knowledge and understanding. He could avoid being accused and arrested.

It is with this knowledge, this burden of human behaviour and an inability to make use of this knowledge, that Dalton knows that he walks without real purpose and sits without real purpose at the house where Ursula and Cornelius are cherished and strangled.

Greyhead, during the years, with his single words never accused anyone in particular. He simply stated facts which could be accepted or ignored.

Dalton lies wishing for the long painful night to end. He questions the reason for the wish. Tears overflow from his swollen eyes. In spite of the mistrust of his fellow lodgers he wishes that those fat, clumsy-looking, but surprisingly gentle fingers could, in their remarkable dance, be wiping away the scalding tears once more. These tears are a familiar part of the bitter taste of the dog kennel. During the discussion group meetings, especially when love between father and son was shuffled from one man to the next, Dalton often recalled without wanting to, the dog kennel. It was with scorn and irritation that he watched his father's pencil stroking and shading with geometrical precision the drawing

Dalton tried to hide from him. Filling in, as his father called it, the walls of the dog kennel, his father explained that the shading should be lightly done in straight lines rather than in a sort of bird's nest, round and round scribbling. For his eleventh birthday one of his presents was a smooth, flat cedarwood box with brass hinges and a little brass lock and key. Nestling in the fragrant compartments were six especially soft pencils, *Venus* B and 2B for sketching. His father, his mouth watering, called them lead pencils, black lead pencils, as only an ignorant Horsefly would.

Later, when his father asked if he could borrow one of the new lead pencils, Dalton, knowing that his father was trying to please him with the request, was unable to remember where the pencils were.

Shivering at times and hot at other times, Dalton moves between pain and sleep and nightmare. His eyes open more easily and, with a curious thankfulness, he looks up to the windows. The inevitable grey morning seems to wait with soft patience outside the row of little high-up windows. The pain, as if departing, hovers now somewhere between these windows and his pillow.

'Mr Foster,' Perce is beside his bed, 'it's not as if we want to but we're obliged to show you your face.' He takes a small cracked mirror from Winch, saying that even if it's an advantage to be beaten up in mud, his nose, as he will see, has been altered.

'Take a look, Mr Foster.' Perce holds the mirror and Dalton, with some difficulty, raises his head and looks at his reflection. The mirror gives an enlarged and grotesque picture of the damage. Dalton hardly recognizes his swollen, discoloured face. His hair is matted with blood. His body is stiff and he cannot stop trembling.

'That shaking,' Perce explains, 'that's weakness.' He tells Winch they must hurry with the bath. They must get Mr Foster moving.

'We'll be one each side of you, Mr Foster,' Perce says. 'We'll walk youse across the landing and then we'll walk youse to the bath. Wench here, he's drawing the hot water now. We'll have to be smart before any busy body lets on to her ladyship what we're up to here in our privacy. We don't want interference just nows.' The two men supporting the third move across slowly.

The sound of the sad horn in the distance approaching the level crossing comes closer. The rumbling of the wheat train is louder and once more the long drawn-out melancholy music of the horn can be heard as it warns at the second level crossing.

Perce and Winch support their nervous and fragile patient. They want to show him something beautiful they tell him again. They move slowly, step by step.

The room across the landing is flooded now with the rising sun. The brilliance of the morning in this room brings with it the remembered crowing of roosters calling and answering across a shallow valley. It is as if a soft, rushing wind is dispersing the mists of the night over far away fields. It is not difficult, for a moment, to recall hollows and slopes which face the sun, golden in the light, and other places which remain shadowed and damp, cool until the day wears on towards the afternoon.

Surprisingly there are two windows in this room, one looking down on to the street and a narrow one looking along the street eastwards. This narrow window is catching the rosy streaks and curls and the full illumination of the sun. The light which is filling the room is pouring through the single tall pane.

The three men move slowly, all together, across the linoleum towards this window as the train with two heavy engines comes into sight rounding the long curve of railway line.

'Here she comes,' Perce says, as they lean together trembling like willow trees planted, three trees together, for strength and endurance. The morning in the room is changing fast as the magic of the sunrise travels in tremulous shiverings of light, down the pattern of the wallpaper behind them, reflected there as if from a lake.

The wagons of the freight train rumble towards them

and continue on alongside the cyclone-wire fence on the other side of the road. A mile of wagons, or more, it is impossible to count them. They bring with their noise the remembered sound of the wind rushing across the wide paddocks, the steady click click of the windmills; and the parrots, the pink and grey birds swooping and screaming from one homestead, one group of trees to the next. These birds, with their rosy breasts and greedy necks, flying towards the rising sun, swiftly circling in ever-widening rings, their colours changing so that in one minute they form a dense pink cloud and, almost at once, they, screaming, disappear and cannot be heard or seen at all. It is as if these wild and unreachable birds come suddenly out of the fresh clear morning and, just as suddenly, go back into it, leaving the steady windmills clicking, their secret power undisturbed.

The train, as it passes, brings the sunlit, embroidered bark of the trees at the edges of the wheat. It seems to contain and give off the scent of hay and the fragrance of the dried grasses and flowers left over from all the summers of childhood. The train suggests one image after another; fences which need mending and cattle silently raising their heads to stare; the train brings memories of pests and diseases and weeds and thieves. Winch adds to the unspoken list, floods and drought, he tells them, scones and jam and hot tea poured from an enamel tea pot. School buses, he says, weddings, funerals, mothers, sisters and fruit cake. Perce interrupts Winch, explaining to Dalton that Wench, before all his trouble, was a good country boy, 'till life got a holt of him'. He goes on to say that Wench is a true poet, but that life has given him too generously of its infections.

'Mr Foster,' Winch is feverish with the passing of the train and his illness, 'you should see this in the moonlight. Have you ever looked out over the stubble in the moonlight?'

Holding Dalton, as they are, they sway perilously as if on the train.

'Wench!' Perce says. 'Wench, get a holt of yourself. The kettle boils. We'll have strong and black and two sugars each. And then, no kidding, Mr Foster must have his bath.'

Once again, the steam from the hot tea is soothing to Dalton's face, his eyes in particular. With a kettle, life at Mrs Porter's would be greatly improved. He wonders in a feeble and muddled way what has to be done in order to have a kettle and, equally importantly, to have a room with a window.

'Oh, Mr Foster, I do so hope you don't mind accepting stolen goods.' Miss Mallow hovers on the landing outside Dalton's room. She is holding, at arm's length, as if she is too polite to step into a gentleman's bedroom, a plastic bag. 'I had a sort of field day, today,' she explains. 'Someone left part of their shopping behind. It's fruit, do you see? Very good for you, it's oranges. I told the girl, the check-out girl, I would run after the customer. I did run but she was gone so quickly, so here it is, some oranges and a pear which looks just right for eating now ...'

'Don't get up,' Miss Mallow says. 'I heard you walked into a lamp post. You must be in great pain. I am sorry.' With great courage Miss Mallow steps into the room and puts the fruit on the chair by Dalton's bed. 'Don't try and talk,' she continues. 'I can see your face is so dreadfully swollen. You must stay in bed ...'

'The fruit is sheer good fortune,' Miss Mallow says after a short pause while Dalton tries to say some kind of thanks. 'I'd had an unfortunate time previously,' she goes on as if feeling she must offer him some conversation. 'I, by mistake, managed to steal a potato. A raw potato. I don't see so well, don't you know, the potatoes looked like peaches and, in passing, I caught one in my sleeve. It is the ultimate in being homeless when you understand you have no way of cooking a potato. I hear,' she continues, 'that it was dark when you walked into the lamp post. It would have seemed as if the whole world was against you ... Mr Afton, my old headmaster, you know, slipped and fell heavily, one time, and he told me that it seemed to him, then, that several people, parents, mostly mothers, had pushed him from behind, though of course there was absolutely no one there. He simply fell. You see, it was just before the terrible thing, the *accusation*, which did come from some parents about – well, about their children. But the supposed events were said to be from *years* before Mr Afton was at the school. And it was all dragged through the newspapers and quite untrue and by the time this was realised it was too late, the damage had been done. She had, she reminds Dalton, known Mr Afton ever since they were children. He was exemplary and so very kind. As a small boy,' Miss Mallow smiles at the memory, 'Mr Afton sometimes had red jam and breadcrumbs on his cheeks.'

Long after Miss Mallow has gone downstairs Dalton goes on thinking about her. He thinks about her poverty, her hunger and her isolation and he thinks how she will remember the sunlight at the end of the long afternoons and how, on Fridays, after school, she would walk with

Mr Afton, each of them carrying a school case, to the school house where Mrs Afton, waiting for them, poured tea and passed round an ornamental plate with slices of a special coconut cake she always made. And then, a little later, Miss Mallow would walk on to the house where she lodged with a family who, for years, had boarded the lady teachers. Dalton can imagine Miss Mallow's hat as being light in weight and colour, made of some sort of straw. She would have worn it with a little scarf of thin material, perhaps chiffon, mauve or pale blue, twisted round it, just above the broad brim. He has always liked hats, he remembers the heavenly little hats worn by his mother and aunt Dalton. Especially, he remembers, the spring hats, little round cushions of soft material covered with snowdrops or exquisite pink rosebuds made of silk and fashioned into tiny posies. The snowdrops, the fresh green and white flowers, were his favourites. Always fresh and clean, and aunt Dalton's eyes sparkled with mischief behind the tantalising fragments of the veil, this transparent snatch of material which could be raised or lowered at the whim of the owner.

'All of it could have been much worse,' Perce says a few days later. He and Winch take turns to look after

Dalton. 'What I'm saying,' Perce continues, 'what I'm saying is that it's the mud saved you. Anywhere else, a car park or a road outside a pub, you'd have been left for dead. Wench'll be with you later when I go out.'

Dalton, always in the past, shrinking from Winch because of the ugly eruptions in his unhealthy sweating skin, is surprised at the way in which he has come to need and to accept the sick man's gentle attention. Winch, with hardly any equipment, but with confidence, has washed Dalton and cleaned his painful wounds every day. He has devoted himself to boiling the kettle, making either the tea or instant soup hourly to ensure, as he explains, the necessary fluids.

'There's beef or chicken,' he says, five minutes before the hour. 'What'll you have? Pick your choice.'

Dalton, half asleep on the mysteriously prescribed medication obtained by Perce, thinks about Mr Afton's terrible and unnecessary disgrace and how easily his own experience might have matched this. After his own panic following the small and blurred scene in Kings College Chapel there was, instigated by himself, simply a brief and dignified conversation in a quiet room, lined with books, and where a shaft of sunlight lay across the polished surface of a great desk. Dalton was allowed, in a few words, to suggest his own immediate future. His suggestion was met with an unexpected kindness and understanding, no harm had been done, and his own attitude towards himself was a relief to those in judgement. He had not been called upon to explain more. His own sense of responsibility being, he was told, acceptable.

There was then, soon after, a number of persons in charge and there were others, like himself in varying degrees, under sentence with the acceptance of specialist consultation, therapy and rehabilitation.

First there was, among others, a woman in charge. She walked with an importance, a marked lordosis and an authoritative step, a repeated footfall, heels, rapid and firm, heels resounding on the uncovered concrete. Her approach could be heard well in advance. And later there was the officer, Greyhead. He ambled leaning backwards, an almost imperceptible slant accommodating his corpulence and possibly assisting his often laboured breathing.

Dalton, already knowing himself, acquiescing, understanding Greyhead's *recognise yourself*, bowing to his own self-recognition and his reverence for truth, entered hopefully the monosyllabic discipline offered by the owners of the powerful heels, the broad leather belts, the special whistles and the bunches of keys. Surprisingly the woman, in spite of her keys and her footsteps (which sent her subordinates flying in all directions), had a kind expression in her eyes and it seemed, at that time to Dalton, that he had her much-needed approval.

Fostère, mon cher! Grüsse aus Meiringen! As one would expect, Monsieur Perdu expresses himself in delicate phrases and flawless handwriting. *Il faut que jeunesse se passe.* Today *les enfants* intend to conquer the *arête*, notoriously sharp and dangerous. For them it is *comme il faut* to do these things since we make the holidays!

That Mrs Porter should have a postal address is quite natural but, all the same, the address beneath his name on the envelope surprises Dalton. He is not accustomed to receiving correspondence.

Sometimes, while reading and re-reading the postcard and looking at the photograph enclosed in the envelope, Dalton imagines, to the point of thinking, that the little group, *Der Alpenkönig mit zwei Menschenfeinde* as M. Perdu goes on to describe himself and the two of them, Cornelius and Ursula, are actually in the street outside gazing up at the tall narrow window of the room occupied by Perce and Winch. Between this thought and his imagination he knows there is no chance of their being anywhere near. The stamps on the card, blurred as they are with the unreadable postmark, are clearly European.

Next on the card there is a note in Ursula's heavy round handwriting; *Dear Mr Foster, so many mountains, the*

Varder, the Wetter-horn, the Schreck-horn (my favourite), the
Finster-horn-Zermatt and the Matter-horn. I shall not return home
until I have climbed them all. Cornelius wants to add something;
hier ist es unheimlich! C.

The photograph, black and white, is very clear. The
father, the Consul, must have taken it. Ursula's smile is
the smile kept for her father. There they are, the three
of them, Cornelius, Ursula and Monsieur Perdu. M.
Perdu stands between the two children. He has an arm
round each one. They are all dressed in winter clothes,
grouped like three kings, the two young people bearing
gifts in the spread palms of their gloved hands. They
are, all three, looking up and smiling as if seeing him
where he leans still, in the narrow window. It is as if
they continue to smile, as he peers at them, and they
then appear to move, raising their hands higher in their
supplicatory offering. He can see that they are standing
in snow. Their white woollen socks are rolled down to
the ankles. They are wearing long overcoats and Ursula
has a charming fur hat, a ring of soft fur on her delicate
forehead. Her eyes are even prettier beneath this hat. It
is as if she knows, already, that when wearing this hat
her eyes will be clear and beautiful to anyone who looks
at her. Even from the photograph this is apparent.

There is no snow outside Mrs Porter's place.

The wheat train approaching the level crossing is,

Dalton knows, carrying the sun-ripened harvest. The snow is on the other side of the world.

Instead of looking out of the narrow window in the room shared by Perce and Winch, Dalton endlessly examines the photograph. The sight of this happy little scene of health and high spirits makes him feel as if he can hear their laughter. The brother and the sister once again are contriving to be in an intimate embrace, the tutor being the essential link between them. He recalls his visits to the house. He wonders in an idle way what the mother is doing now and saying. He remembers Cornelius, one time, in a squeaky falsetto reciting, while seated at his tapestry, a litany of embroidery, montmellick, he said then, crewel work, Berlin woolwork, *gros point*, *petit point*, needle painting, ribbon work, bead work, black work and the elegant tambour ... His mother and Ursula had thrown cushions at him, even M. Perdu had joined in, lazily selecting a small cushion and tossing it without any real intention.

In the photograph the two young people are holding out their hands as if in an act of perpetual offering. Perhaps, Dalton thinks, they are offering mercy or pity or love, intangible gifts since their well-gloved hands are not actually holding anything. It is like having a new book to read, this speculation on the details offered in the photograph. And then there are other possible thoughts about the unseen mother and the unseen father and their unseen lives.

'I'll have a catafalque especially erected.' Winch comes to the end of a coughing fit with this statement, adding that it would be for himself. His remark interrupts Dalton's fantasy with the photograph.

'And a velvet baldachin,' Winch says, 'a suitable place …' His cough, overtaking him, causes him to struggle for breath.

'You'll have a watter watt?' Perce says. 'You and your night school!'

'And,' Winch persists, 'like the great philosopher, Neechey, I'll have a holy priest to pray over my dead body. This man, Neechey,' Winch goes on, 'said he didn't want a priest or any kind of religious service, but his sister ignored his last wishes and so he was prayed over and his coffin was surrounded with candles *and* incense *and* silver crosses *and* flowers *and* prayers. That's what I'll have.'

Dalton, unable to answer, regards Winch with a silence which causes him to feel ashamed. Of course there would be no silences in the classrooms at the night school. The Cambridge silences would be quite unknown to Winch and could make him feel small and insignificant.

In the continuing silence Perce, clearing his throat, speaks: 'You and your reading books, Wench!' Dalton hears the tremble in Perce's voice. He too clears his throat as if to hide and push aside the thoughts of the corridor of little wards in the hospital, all of them with their doors open but, frequently, a door is closed upon the silence within.

A particularly unpleasant pneumonia perhaps, and too many visitors, edging each other, apologising for coming but crowding in all the same. Masses of flowers and the visitors saying, *insisting* that they know they have come at the wrong time yet staying far too long when there are not enough chairs and, in any case, not enough space for chairs. Then the flowers, piling up, droop over the wash basins. Other considerations are the sore arms, painful from injections and transfusions, and the rattle of ice cubes on stainless steel for mouths burning with infection. All the reproachings and the distress and the impossibilities of explanation or of healing are in the little heaps of decorative paper vomit bowls piled up on the locker tops.

Dalton thinks that Winch will not be burdened with visitors. His mother was alone in bed when her heart failed. There was no bedside visit for her, neither was there one for aunt Dalton who was tied, for her own safety, in a chair. As she had no idea who Dalton was or where she was, he never went back. He was the only visitor (by special arrangement, as when he visited aunt Dalton) at his father's bedside.

It is not possible to know, the thoughts cross Dalton's mind, if the nurses welcome visitors or not. Perhaps these silent nurses in their gowns and latex gloves find their work from one tiny ward to the next simpler if there are no visitors in the way. Or, alternatively, a breath from beyond the doors and windows of the hospital might be a restorative.

'You and your reading books, Wench,' Perce repeats in a firm voice. 'I'm off for hot chips. Put the kettle on, Wench.'

It is clear to Dalton that, without saying anything, Perce knows, and Winch knows, that soon Winch will be in need of all that they can do to help him. Meanwhile he has recovered from the coughing which seems to consume completely while it lasts.

'Here,' Dalton says, getting up with stiff movements. 'Here,' he regrets his silence earlier, 'let me do the kettle for a change.'

'The wound,' Winch says after a pause, 'the idea is that the suffering in the lives of artists and writers has a deep connection with creativity.'

'Oh you!' Dalton says. 'You and your night school...'

Sein Blick ist vom Vorübergehn der Stäbe
so müd geworden, dass er nichts mehr hält.
Ihm ist, als ob es tausend Stäbe gäbe
und hinter tausend Stäben keine Welt.

His gaze from going through the bars has
grown so weary that it can take in nothing more.
For him it is as though there were a
thousand bars and behind the thousand bars no world.

'The Panther'
R. M. RILKE

✎

'I felt so embarrassed, I did reelly,' Miss Vales tells Mrs Porter. 'Reelly I did. There I was waiting at the edge of the underground car park, waiting for the toilet. The ladies' toilet was being cleaned by a *man*. I mean, there were two men and this big metal trolley in the doorway and the mop as well and people passing by and *me waiting*.

' "Sorry about keeping youse ladies waiting," the one man says, just as if he *knows*. Embarrassing, *and* I'm the *only one waiting*.'

'Never you mind, EV,' Mrs Porter says, 'it's all in a day's work for them. Now, EV, *here is Mr Foster*. See who's here, it's Mr Foster.' With a capable hand, attached to a monstrous arm, Mrs Porter detains and holds Dalton Foster as he attempts, already dressed in his raincoat, to slide out of the dining room to reach the front door without having to walk across the hall which is well blocked by Mrs Porter. For a moment the three of them are wedged in an inescapable bunch.

Mrs Porter tells them she has a surprise. She will not keep them in suspense. It is a beautiful surprise. It is the wedding of two of the loveliest people walking on God's earth. Truly two people, two beautiful people, standing right there, with her, in her very own hall. Two people who should *share* each other, no other than these two lovely people themselves.

'Miss Vales is no whippet.' Mrs Porter makes the announcement to Mr Foster who can see that he is obliged to drop his recent ambition. Miss Vales nudges Mrs Porter; 'Oh, go on with you,' she says with a series of self-conscious little squeals.

'She might not be as young as she was and that's the honest truth.' Mrs Porter, as if describing something in the cattle yard at an agricultural show, keeps a strong grip on both Dalton Foster and Miss Vales. 'She'll not give you any trouble, Mr Foster. I'll be plain with you. I need the room, *your* room. What with rates and taxes I'll be on my ear. But with Mr Right and Mrs Right here under the same ceiling ...' Mrs Porter, filled with emotion within, pauses to hug her own bosom and to give herself time to control her feelings. She adds a few words, expressing pride and pleasure in having the wedding celebration on her own premises.

Miss Vales bursts into hysterical tears and Mr Foster, taken completely by surprise, gulps and nods as if he has suddenly been expected to ask the Lord's Blessing for a meal at an unfamiliar table. He makes for the stairs, his legs and his body in one long agonized contortion, leaving his raincoat in Mrs Porter's generous hands. He is unable, in this moment, to provide the polite invention of fiction, the excuse which would excuse him indefinitely and which would heal, for ever, the harm, a previously unthought of harm, that of an unchivalrous act, a sin which he had no intention of committing.

It is a question he tells himself, when safely in his room with the door closed, *of changing the destroyed inner self into something optimistic and capable of human warmth.* His thoughts do not entirely surprise him. His recent experiences, he is intelligent enough to know, have brought about considerable change in him. Speech still deserts him when it is most needed, but even that can be an advantage. One awkward utterance might be more reason for future endless disentangling.

He tries to apply creative thought to Mrs Porter's extraordinary suggestion, but is only able to tell himself that he should have left earlier. He has been lingering, foolishly, a little longer in the dining room, at the inhospitable breakfast table, where Mrs Disley, waiting to clear, holds forth some mornings on the state of the world. This morning she had described a row of derelict small shops, one a Jewish tailor's place, very small — next to a run-down newsagent's, next to that, a sandwich bar and a video library next to the sandwich place, all in readiness, she explained to her audience of one, for the demolition. Just around the corner, apparently, from the Station Road, a stone's throw from Mrs Porter's place. The Homeless, she told Mr Foster, are nearer than you think; 'They have taken over these shops, just children they are,' she explained, 'just children with shit for brains, living in the filthy rooms over those empty shops, fucking each other stupid, tearing up the floorboards and burning them of a night time to keep warm. I mean, who do they think they are?' Mrs Disley, the self-appointed custodian of local squalor, possessed a voice which carried indignation magnificently. 'Picture them,' she went on, 'dropping on perfect strangers, innocent people, mind you, punching them up for their money, elderly gents such as yourself, with more manners than sense or money, just for a coupla dollars. *And* they're *blatant*. Walking into shops and helping theirselves to apples and milk and bread, anythin' they can get their hands on. *And* there was a sign, ever so rude it was.' Mrs Disley had paused as if this was too delicate to mention and then, warming to her subject, empty toast-racks swinging on her red fingers, she continued, 'a rude sign, there was, on the boarded-up front of the tailor's shop. Done in chalk it was, saying that the Bloody Cows in the Crisis Centre should pull their fingers out and stop wasting other people's time. What do these children want with *time*!' Mrs Disley wanted to know. 'What do they do all day that they want time for it? If you arsk me,' she said, changing tone, 'it's the split homes, no mothers, and the dads aren't any better. Ask any boy what he talks about with his dad. They don't talk. All a boy can expect from his dad is a coupla curses and a belting and all a father can expect from his son is insolence ...'

Jolted by the unexpected exaggerated reference to his age and caught in this river of hyperbole, Dalton, feeling since his recent experience, anxious for both parents and children and perhaps, even more so for himself, had made for the door and, stepping from the raging floodwaters, the torrents of Disley, the phrase formed itself in his mind, into the tidal reaches of an entirely different river flowing beyond in the hall he, in desperation, had been forced to make what must have appeared to be a rude and careless leap to the staircase.

What was it Heraclitus had said about rivers? Temporarily, in the seclusion and the silence of his seemingly windowless room, he waits pressed close to the door until he is able to feel it will be safe to go downstairs and leave the house, as usual, by the front door. Mrs Porter will most certainly have left his raincoat on one of the hooks in the hall.

She calls it having sex. She says men have to have sex. She knows this. Don't ask her she says she just knows it Mr F she says Mr F did you know? Mr F she keeps on this Mr F listen to this Mr F Mr F I must tell you Mr F just you listen to this. Listen! She starts everything she says with listen. And if it isn't Mr F it's Mrs Porter Mrs Porter says Mrs Porter believes Mrs Porter ...

Dalton Foster, driving the hired car with the special care of one who, at a rather late age, has recently obtained a licence but has not had much practice, allows himself the consolation of being quietly, in his thoughts, irritated.

'Some men, Mr F,' his companion in the passenger seat reiterates, returning as if to previous thoughts of her own, or worse as if reading his mind, 'some men have to have sex. It's part of their body they have to have it, no matter what. I do know this. But I do know too,' she makes as if snuggling closer to the uncompromising space between them, 'that sex isn't everything. I've always been broadminded, but. Mrs Porter's always telling me: "The trouble with you EV," Mrs Porter says if she's said it once she's said it a dozen times; "The trouble with you EV is that you're too broadminded."

Oops! There! I've snagged my nylons there on the four in the floor. What a giggle ...'

The sharp scent, previously unfamiliar but now all too well known to Dalton, of nail varnish, fills the confined space between the front seats and the dashboard as the new Mrs Dalton Foster sets about a hungry-fingered, nimble dabbing at the tiny ruptures in her new stockings. 'Mrs Porter, you know,' the new Mrs Dalton Foster says, 'Mrs Porter always said that Mr Right would turn up for me eventually. "EV" she would say, "sure as I'm sitting here with this tea pot, Mr Right is waiting just out there around the corner. He's here as large as life in these tea leaves. I see him plain. He's closer than you think." And, did you know, I never ever reelly ever thought Mr Right would be you? It's a laugh, it reelly is. You and me. Well, we're not a bit alike, are we? Attractions of the opposites that's what Mrs Porter said.'

Heraclitus said that all things flow, it is not possible to step in the same river twice. Dalton Foster is accustomed to the swift and silent movement of his mind. As the car travels through the summer-brown countryside, the cows in the paddocks, on both sides of the road, do not raise their heads. They are occupied with their own shortsighted view of the bleached grass. Heraclitus, Dalton seeks further consolation in thought, Heraclitus did not add that images of things are even more fleeting. Images, he warms privately to his theme, images change with the maker of them – whether he is in good health, whether he is tired or hungry or disappointed. Images, he allows himself one final internal pronouncement, are essentially personal. Dalton is both tired and hungry and, he supposes, he is not disappointed so much as profoundly depressed. Surrounded, as he feels he is by acres of unendurable boredom, he envies the cows their acres of poor feed. Being unable to get away from the source of the boredom is similar to being in prison. During the journey while his companion is talking endlessly with a happiness that is frightening about bathrooms – I reely like matching towels and pillow cases, you know embroidered HIS and HERS – and on to bedroom suites, designer wardrobes, fashion silk jackets and scarves, Trax and Reeboks with blow ups ... he watches the passing scenes of unknown townships, all with ramshackle buildings and verandah posts crazy enough to have been put there recently for a shoot out in a Western. He notices that each place has its own hotel, its own petrol station, and a storage tank, a silo, a railway siding and what looks like obsolete farm machinery alongside the road. He cannot help noticing, too, the frightening lack of evidence of attempts to ameliorate the heat which could be even worse than it is at present.

'I mean,' the new Mrs Foster remarks, following his troubled gaze with her own eyes and changing the subject, trying to be a part of his unspoken thoughts, coming upon them yet again with unexpected insight, 'all those tin roofs out there and not a bit of shade.'

Mr Foster, though he has never wanted to be married himself, has often thought that it would be comfortable to have someone to come back to, perhaps to talk things over with and to exchange anecdotes, or to notice and mention things like: darker patches on ceilings, or wallpaper which is perfectly hideous, or to be able to say things like: 'isn't Mrs Porter absolutely dreadful' and then to laugh with that other person. But he knows that he did not want a wife. The word wife suggests all kinds of unmentionable things.

'I do so like a nice bathroom,' the new Mrs Foster is insisting. 'I know Mrs Porter says people put all their money into their bathrooms and you don't live in a bathroom and having more than one makes more to clean, but I have seen some lovely bathrooms, you know, black and gold and marble, all mirrors too and telephones at the places where I go baby-sitting, and some places have ducky little bathrooms specially for their children and then there's bathrooms for visitors. All the same I've always felt comfortable in the bathroom at Mrs Porter's. I've always liked the green painted floor, wood you know, and in the mornings the sun comes right in there, makes it seem somehow cosy and freshens you up if you've been at someone's place all night – baby-sitting ...'

It is certainly not possible to laugh about Mrs Porter with the new Mrs Foster. Mr Foster tries instead to think of books, of the pleasure of dying surrounded by books, the window-sills piled high with books *arranged three by three* with books. He tries to remember something he read once, years ago when he was a student, about books *keeping watch like angels with outspread wings* and being like an image or a sign of resurrection.

'There was a man crushed to death, it was in the paper, crushed to death he was by books. A bookcase fell on him while he was choosing a book to take to bed. Imagine!' The new Mrs Foster said, the evening before, when she saw the little pile of reading material he had prepared for their journey.

'Imagine what it would be like to have all books falling on you, you'd suffocate. Didn't you read about the man crushed to death? It said in the paper he'd written some of them himself. Just goes to show, Mrs Porter said it was a judgement.'

The motel, for the first night of their honeymoon, is hard to find being set back from the main road and dark, hidden in trees. An immediate inspection, while Mr Foster is still clutching the key on its little painted board, reveals heavy dust-laden curtains hanging without any possibility of being drawn back. The curtains cover the full length of the windows which resemble shop windows in size and thickness but having nothing displayed, he discovers, except the ugly side wall of the next unit. The fixed furniture bothers him. It is not possible to move the table or the chairs, and there is no door between the living space and the bedroom. This worries him too, as does the unforgettable and inescapable smell of frying, of sausages burst and burned and stuck in the pan, a legacy from the previous occupants. He feels himself responsible for a certain amount of chivalry.

'Miss Vales,' he says at the end of their industrious and uneasy examination, 'I noticed upon arrival that there is a restaurant attached to this motel.' The new Mrs Foster, accustomed to being called Miss Vales for a great many years of her life, does not seem to see any reason for correction. She settles, with delight, in front of the dingy mirror, patting and teasing her new perm, turning her head first to one side and then the other.

With some extra pullings and twistings she manages, Mr Foster thinks, with great skill to aid the extraordinary pile of hair to maintain its erection. Women's hair, he comes to the conclusion, seems to be either a gleaming metallic tower of smooth impenetrable brilliance or it is a mass of ropes and coils indescribably tangled, sometimes drawn back from the face but mainly, like deadly poisonous creepers in pictures of rain forests, hanging over and obliterating features and expression completely. Both are equally impervious. Miss Vales's edifice, he notices, is inclined to lean.

The motel is cool but depressing. The path which leads to the beach turns out to be long and its dreary curves are well supplied with tins and bottles and litter of a more personal sort. Flies and mosquitoes are in abundance. The idea of a walk before dinner is abandoned quickly.

They are the only guests in the darkened dining room. Seeing their self-conscious reflections in the cave of gold-edged mirrors, Dalton thinks, during the meal, that he is the more pathetic in appearance. He feels sorry for Miss Vales, all the more so at the beginning of the meal when she managed to be excited and quite noisily frivolous about a decision of the menu.

'Oh, Mr F, you choose and order.' He feels he will never forget the desperation behind the apparently light-hearted request. Gulping, he had glanced up at the waitress, a red-cheeked country girl who settled the problem by saying, 'There's only the tuna and sweet corn mornay tonight. Everything's off excepting that.'

⁂

'Well, Mr F, tomorrow's motel might be quite different and there might be a moon, you can never tell, it takes all sorts.' The new bride chatters mercilessly, back once more, perched before the mirror, patting and teasing all over again her hair, turning her head from side to side as she studies her own reflection. Keeping her knees together she slides, under the covers lying down near the edge of the bed as gingerly as Mr Foster, buttoned in his new pyjamas, does on his side. She begins to explain about her headache almost at the moment when he is wondering how best to announce his.

⁂

Mr Dalton Foster wishes now during the night that he had taken Miss Vales back into the town for dinner. Though he was unfamiliar and nervous then, he is sure now that there would have been a better restaurant there. He wishes too that he could open the heavy curtains or loop them over a chair and then he remembers all the furniture is immovable. Even the padded stool, his new wife's favourite perch, in front of the dressing table is a fixture. A fat woman could easily become wedged in the small space. Mrs Porter for example. The constant chatter about Mrs Porter during the day has made him feel that he has only to stretch out his hand to open his door at Mrs Porter's place. Or that he could meet Perce and Winch if he walked outside, or Miss Mallow, in the way he is used to meeting them on the stairs or in the hall. Sometimes, lying in bed in his room at Mrs Porter's, he could hear Miss Mallow playing, with over use of the soft pedal, the piano parts of the Saint-Saëns piano concerto.

'It's Saint-Saëns,' she told him once without being asked, at the foot of the stairs. 'It's Saint-Saëns piano concerto number two.' She told him then that she seemed to hear the orchestra in her head and then was able to come down with emphasis on the piano. She told him too that she often tried to sing the orchestral melody and harmony aloud but the sound which came out was never the same as it was in her head. He knew from what he was able to hear that on some days she did not even raise the shabby blistered lid. He knew, without seeing the piano, just how the veneer had come off in places. Until recently, she told him once, she had not noticed how old it looked. The sound, she explained then, did not matter. It had never mattered even when the older girls at the school practised their sonatas, their études, their sarabands and their marches. It had seemed to her then, she said, as if the ancient instrument had a certain charm, reminiscent of some authentic masterpiece made by a craftsman in musical contrivances. 'The vibration of the strings,' Miss Mallow lowered her voice as if in reverence, 'produced sound then almost similar to that of the harpsichord. Clementi,' she continued, her voice lower still, 'Clementi was said to be the Father of the modern pianoforte playing. *And*,' Mr Foster remembers her smile as she went on, '*and*, I like to think that my piano could be said to resemble an instrument made and played by this great man.'

Mr Foster, moving his stiff legs with caution on his side of the bed, tries not to breathe. It is not possible for him to know if his bride, the word does not come easily to him, is asleep. As she is not chattering he presumes that she is.

Once at Mrs Porter's, Miss Mallow, peering from her door as if waiting for him, waylaid him in the hall.

'It's the small things I take,' she said. 'Only the small things. Small things which will slide from my pocket into the lining of my coat, a bread roll, a tea bag in its envelope, a tiny three-cornered cheese wrapped in foil, an egg lifted carefully from a carton of eggs, a small chocolate bar, a tomato and perhaps an onion. Not all at once,' she assured him, 'because, you know, there are special people who watch for thieves. I never thought, you know, that I would be a thief. You understand, don't you, you see I have to find a little supper somewhere. I have never told anyone about all this. I never thought I would sit, without money, waiting on the benches in the arcade where the supermarket is. When I'm back in my room at Mrs Porter's, I tell Mr Afton everything. Mr Afton was my old headmaster. He it was gave me the piano. I tell him things all the time, in my head, you understand . . .'

Thinking about Miss Mallow during this long uncomfortable night, Dalton Foster can see clearly that there is really not much difference between her future and his except that he has more money, not much more, than she has. And, of course, he is married and she is not. The marriage, as it is, he feels does not make all that much difference. The difference, if there is one, is chiefly that though he is ignorant, naïve perhaps, he is not innocent as she is. Trying not to turn over and so disturb the silent Miss Vales, he reminds himself of something he read years ago in a literary paper. Unable to remember the exact words he recalls the essence, which was that life has stipulations from which certain requirements spring. Life, he thinks, in its bleakness does not hold much for Miss Mallow or Miss Vales or himself.

The honeymoon, like the wedding, had been Mrs Porter's idea. He supposes that she meant well but the thought of spending the money he is really unable to afford, the thought of the future, even a second night in a motel is appalling apart from everything else. Mrs Porter made it clear that three nights were the minimum acceptable for a honeymoon.

'Three nights, EV, he owes you three.' Mrs Porter held up three large fingers; even in his presence she did this and he remained silent. Silence during the years had become his way and there did not seem any possibility of changing this.

'I mean,' Mrs Porter said, 'you can't go away for less. Where in Gawd's name can you get to in less? And then you've to get back, haven't you? You can't get anywhere in one day.' Mr Foster's silence was, he understands, regarded as an acquiescence. He is deeply sorry now. Sorry for Miss Vales because he is silently irritated with her the whole time. He is sorry that he has no qualities fitting for a bridegroom. His dealings with women have always been mainly by accident.

'I've been talking to a lady on the telephone,' he told his aunt when she asked him what he had been doing.

'Who could our precious child have been talking to?'

aunt Dalton and his mother pondered. They really wanted to know.

'He is *excited*,' aunt Dalton said. 'See how flushed his little face is. And look at his eyes, they're bright. Perhaps he's feverish.' His aunt and his mother, deciding that he was, put him to bed immediately in his mother's room.

'You know,' his aunt said, 'it must have been the operator. He must have called the operator simply by accident.' The two women enjoyed reasoning. 'Perhaps he'll do other things by accident.' They seemed then to be cautiously considering an uncertain future while at the same time brushing and arranging each other's hair, bunching the curls holding them up and back, exposing on each neck the soft white nape.

'Bone or grosgrain?' aunt Dalton questioned, while selecting the ornamental hair bands. 'This corded silk, this greeny black silk, like the arched tail feathers of a young cock, my dear, is striking and very strong but, see, the bone is irresistable, smooth and simple, absolutely aesthetic, very dependable, a certain generator of clear penetrating thought. Which will you ...?' The laughter, starting as a soft breathless whispering and a catching of breath, began to change as Dalton lay encircled by the two women, their arms reaching across caressing each other so that immediately above him their breasts, escaping the soft folds of clothing, naked and scented, caught him lightly as they moved, touching and nudging his face and his lips till he too was caught up in the long low sigh, the forerunner of the magic of exquisite sensation.

Mr Foster, hardly breathing, raises himself. The smallish mound on the other edge of the bed makes no movement. Miss Vales could be dead for all that she is so still. He feels his way, with all the stealth of a thief, to the tiny bathroom. It occurs to him that Miss Vales might be lying there under the covers awake and prepared to endure with absolute silence the whole long night. There were people who would do this sort of thing. They would sit something out. It is not his sort of phrase but then this night, this whole journey and the reason for it, is not his sort of thing . . .

'Predator and libertine no more!' Winch made the announcement upon hearing the news of Mr Foster's imminent and supposedly adventitious marriage. Winch went on to say that he had read about arranged marriages.

'Like in India,' he said. 'It's the best way to be married, these marriages last *for ever*. No more chasing after ...' His cough stopped him then from saying more.

Dalton, setting out very early in the morning, is contemplating a secret, cautious walk, a long walk of permanent escape. A walk from which he has no intention of returning. Reeboks, dreadlocks, bejewelled noses and wrap-around sunglasses; he has, during the chatter of his wife, been trying to accustom himself to change. Mostly it seems that his life has been, repeatedly, this very same attempt.

It is still dark. The birds are still silent. As he walks on the soft sand of the track his footsteps make no sound. He walks away from the motel. He can hear the soft snoring of the sea close behind him. At intervals there is a subdued crash of waves as they gather to reach a little further up the beach. The tide, with its restrictions, is coming in. He knows he is the victim of change, especially with this last event, his wedding and the first night of marriage spent, without sleep, beside his bride who possibly did not sleep either. Changes are a part of life, he tells himself.

'Predator and libertine no more.' He thinks now about Winch. It has always been his custom to turn his thoughts elsewhere, a self-created method of consolation in the face of sorrow or disappointment and, he has discovered, it is a way of surviving. It would be a mistake, he knows, to question the benefits of survival. Instead he thinks about Winch. One of the changes to be realised is the change in Winch, an expected but distressing and not wanted change. Suddenly Winch is thin, much more so than before, raw-boned and, after Perce's recent shaving and hairdressing, looks scraped about the jaws and head. Winch is in hospital again for something they call *tests* and a *fill-up*. Perce, visiting, spends all his time sitting beside Winch in the hospital ward. He massages Winch gently, his painful legs, his shoulders and his elbows. Dalton, visiting, arrived one time just as Perce was bringing Winch, exhausted, back to his bed from the shower where Perce had washed him and had washed his head, even though one of the nurses had advised against this.

Winch would be back at Mrs Porter's soon enough,

Perce explained then, even though it was a particularly unpleasant bronchitis type of thing. There was no need to visit, Perce said, Winch would be back within a few days. Dalton wondered immediately whether he had inadvertently shown horror or distaste in his expression but Perce merely went on to warn him against walking in the suburbs or in the park as he had been accustomed to doing. 'And I mean the river as well,' Perce said. He might easily be recognized, Perce said, in spite of, or because of, the badly discoloured scars on his face and the damaged nose which, though it altered his appearance completely, might be recognised by those whose artistic handiwork it was.

'It fairly suits you, in any case.' Perce, looking worn out, had taken the small amount of money Dalton shyly offered, suggesting that Perce could buy something Winch would feel able to eat. Perce, pocketing the gift, was certain he would be able to find the very thing in the market.

Dalton's walk is a long walk. The darkness changes to that half light before dawn. The country on both sides is hidden in a rising mist. There is a sweet fragrance of grass. Reaching the main road he takes the direction back to town, not to Mrs Porter's place, not to the park and not to the house. A letter from Monsieur Perdu has explained that the whole family will be moving from the house. The Consul is being posted. Cornelius and Ursula, with their mother and himself, are once again on holiday. Another family will take over the substantial brick house. M. Perdu, in his letter, expresses sorrow that they have to part with the pleasure of Mr Foster's company. The letter came the day before the wedding; it is crumpled in Dalton's raincoat pocket. Another family will breathe the dust in the haphazard, out-of-date library. The chair covers and the curtains of flowered chintz, whether they are liked or not, will persist. He hopes that a postcard will come from Ursula and Cornelius, perhaps a photograph as well, from Rome or Budapest or Paris. These are the places longed for, at one time, by his mother and aunt Dalton. The children's mother, the kind indefatigable mother, Dalton feels sure she will enjoy her travelling with enormous energy. He supposes that the fine line of attraction, this thread which seems unbreakable, will continue to bind the brother and the sister ...

As he walks, long fingers of light lie along the horizon and various shapes appear along the roadside; trees and scrub make grotesque human gestures. And, in a corner of a paddock, a group of silent cows raise their heads slowly as Dalton passes.

On the morning of his wedding day Mrs Porter, blocking the passage, and taking Dalton on one side as he tried to escape unseen from the dining room, told him that, for his own good and for the sake of his marriage, he should play Bingo.

'For your health, believe you me,' Mrs Porter said.

Surprising himself with tears, and Mrs Porter without words, Dalton wanted to explain to her, and to anyone, that he had not undergone a lengthy and expensive education in order to spend his last years playing this game, this silly empty game.

As he walks Dalton tries to put together phrases for possible writing. *Writing is rhythm and cadence*, he says the words aloud, surprised at the nervous trembling voice which is his voice. This is how people would hear him if he spoke. *There is consolation*, he continues, making his voice louder, *there is consolation and healing in saved images*. He is unable to remember whether this is something he has been told or whether he has read it somewhere. For some reason he is crying, his face is wet with tears. The tears blur the tiny slice of radiance beneath the storm cloud, left, as the night sky peels itself away.

❧

Frequently on their little journey Miss Vales took out what she insisted on calling the wedding snaps.

'They're ever so nice,' she said, while they sipped pale coffee from foam cups in a road-house. 'Some lovely ones of Mrs Porter. And here's one of Miss Mallow having a little cry. You have to have someone cry at your wedding, Mrs P says so. And here's one of the floor show. What a giggle, Mr F, take a look.' She passed him picture after picture across the horrible little table. 'The floor show,' she said. 'Pootsie, Trotter and Slem, here's another with them dressed up as bridesmaids. Just look at their little handbags and the posies, so pretty they are those boys! Oh, and here's the table with everything matching, powder blue. I love blue, it's a lucky colour, powder-blue candles, blue cake icing, blue table cloth and blue serviettes ...' (Dalton found himself flinching at the word *serviettes*, he could hear aunt Dalton's scorn and his mother's laughter.)

It was a funny thing about photographs. Dalton, reflecting on the wedding pictures remembers that, in all of them for some reason, either his back or the back of his head must have been towards the camera. And, in one of them, it looked as if he was furtively walking out of the picture; and in another he was slipping out sideways.

It is as if he can see, all over again, Miss Vales' thin excited face and her thin fingers handling the photographs. Even in her happiness her eyes never lost the look of strain and anxiety. Dalton could imagine her alone in that lonely place, the ugly motel in the dark scrub. She would understand at once that he had left her. She might be weeping hopelessly just at this present time. Tears gather again in his own eyes and he searches his pockets for the handkerchief she had given him when they were setting off.

His expensive education, the phrase troubles him. He had not meant to throw the words and their implied meaning at Mrs Porter. The only excuse he has now is that her ludicrous suggestions had taken him by surprise. It is not in his nature, he knows, to wish harm to come to anyone. All the same, his education and his upbringing were not intended to make his life more difficult and distressing as time passed. If Miss Vales is sitting, crying alone in the dreary motel room, in spite of any reasoning, intelligent reasoning, he has to admit to himself it is more than partly his fault. Mrs Porter and Miss Vales, themselves, being too stupid to be considered completely fallible.

It seems that the thin legs of the little girl dance ahead of him still as he walks the lonely night-time road. In spite of, or perhaps because of the brutal ending to this previous dream, he is still able to bring the image of the wished for little companion to his mind. He easily remembers how she hopped back and forth, running with a nimble skill between the lines of traffic. She ran without care as if it could not matter if her life ended abruptly in the severe pain of an accident. It always seemed to him then, as now, that the presence of a child in his life suggested seclusion and safety. And then there was all the warmth and fragrance and childish noise which children unpack around themselves to their own advantage, wherever they happen to be. He changes his thought with an efficiency gained from experience.

The great power is in the lover. Socrates was said to have made such an announcement, meaning that in becoming the lover, rather than the beloved, there was an assumption of supreme ownership; the lover hovering endlessly, in perfect control, above and on all sides of the beauty of the beloved. A curious discipline of thinking comes with the thoughts as they spread with extraordinary rapidity to summon images which, if they bring pain, bring consolation as well. This gift, which Dalton has cherished, contains specific recipes for the needed images. One such repeated consoling thought was of the boy soprano, who, in his infancy with all the tenderness about him as of a special plant, an aromatic, thin-stemmed herb, followed him to his door. Dalton now, as he has often done since then, recalls opening the door to the delicate invitation which seemed then to carry all the experience of the superb perfection of the double harmony of singing and the arriving unexpectedly, yet with expectation, to the complete and erotic satisfaction of the final note. Instead of following the boy now in his thought, he imagines easily the boy in preparation for the offering of this invitation.

The boy, finding himself in the dormitory alone at a time during the day when this long shabby room is deserted, parades before the tarnished mirror at the far end of the room. With his small undergarments rolled down into a thin line of cloth just below the hips, the child examines his own nakedness, comparing himself with his own reflections, twisting his thin, clean little body in an act of childish homage to his own fragile beauty.

The consoling, and at the same time troublesome, image comes sharply once more in the recollection of the small step, without beginning and without end, to that place in the calm, sun-filled shaft of colour directly below the stained glass of the holy window.

In the middle of the road, at the top of a slight rise, Dalton stops walking. The game of catching up with his father was always a part of the ritual of falling asleep. During the years he, secretly, kept alive the idea that his father was ahead of him, walking on a road which was wet, shining after a heavy shower. Now, as the mist is disappearing, if someone was ahead of him, he would be seen clearly on this long stretch of empty road. If he walked faster he might really overtake his father this time and so be able to say to him the words he wanted to say. In reality, he knows that the only way in which his father can be near is in thought and memory. He understands that he brings in the painful thoughts as a counter irritant, as one of aunt Dalton's remedies, a mustard plaster or an enticing and spiteful piece of gossip, might be used to dull a pain already in possession of a particular part of the body or the mind. The thought of 'catching up' with his father is recognisable as a way of putting the painful thoughts of Miss Vales into second place. Dalton finds a few moments of comfort in remembering Hippocrates and his observation about the nature of pain; this being that when there are two pains in the body, the more violent pain can lessen the other one. A parallel to this theory lies in an even more pertinent truth, that a second sorrow might sometimes alleviate, temporarily, a first sorrow.

It is unbearable now to imagine Miss Vales in her bleak isolation, perhaps with all the wedding photographs spread out on the ugly fixed table, her eyes red and swollen with weeping and her hair neglected. He feels helpless in the face of his own actions and behaviour.

A rigid intellectual integrity is not enough in human relationships. He understands this. He regrets, with a rush of bitter sadness, that he has walked away, leaving her alone. What does a bride do? What can she do when her husband leaves her on her wedding night?

As he walks on, the same thoughts keep turning over in his mind. He is unable to forget her attempts to make him feel at ease. And then there was her courage, her brave happiness, especially during the evening meal, their dinner, in the presence of his silence, his complete lack of response. She must, he realises, have noticed his silence, his way of not replying to her remarks which he thought, at the time, were random and incredibly stupid. With another surprising rush of sadness he understands that she, out of her depths, was trying to be, quite simply, nice to him. It is clear that since he knows her insignificance and since she has not the slightest knowledge or understanding of him, he is the one who should be in the position of responsibility. He should be looking after her. He should be making allowances and thinking of her well being and happiness.

❦

'Knock me down with ten feathers EV. What on Gawd's earth didjoo do after you both had your dinners EV?' It is as if he hears Mrs Porter's questioning voice

234

climbing higher with every word of indignation.

'And when EV if I may arsk when didjoo realise the bridegroom had gorn? Hit me in the eye with a burning fence post EV. I mean did he go orf straight away or what? I mean did he *linger*...?'

Mrs Porter at least must give way to father. His father would have hastened to make Miss Vales feel welcome. He would have insisted on her having the most comfortable chair. He would, with his customary good manners, have drawn her into conversation, asking her opinion on the qualities of tea or of hair brushes, that sort of thing, causing her to feel appreciated. He would have recollected, for Miss Vales, an amusing account of Dalton's pet rabbit hopping between the gravy-boat and the vegetable dishes; or perhaps a description of the remembered little bridge and the paper boats, and how easily they came to grief and how this did not really matter since it was only a game ...

Deeply ashamed, he faces the truth that there is nothing for him in his life left over from those earlier times of careless and ardent loving; there is nothing of the delightful laziness, the pretence of scholarship, during the long summer evenings on the green banks of the river at Cambridge. And there is no company of beautiful young men and women, graceful in their summer clothes, walking and sitting and lying on the soft lawns, exchanging thoughts and ideas and thinking themselves brilliant in each other's youthful eagerness. He has to understand that his life was, in several ways, cut off then and it cannot be resumed – as it was.

In the middle of the road Dalton stops walking once more. He turns and walks back along the way he has come.

He is walking now as quickly as he can. The sunrise beneath the stormy sky lights up the tops of the trees and enhances the deep, winter green of the roadside paddocks. This is a different time in his life. Perhaps this one time he will be able to make a choice. It is as if he is able, once more to choose. He feels excited. His legs tremble and his eyes fill with tears. He will be able to make a selection of little cakes and have them neatly placed on a lacy paper mat in a special cake box. There is, all at once, a possibility of a careless happiness, a home coming with his selection in the special box suspended, by a loop of pink string, on one finger.

He remembers a road-house, not the one with the pale luke-warm coffee in the foam cups, but another one close to the motel. They will certainly have something in their oven warmer or whatever they call it. They are open all hours, he remembers the notice welcoming *all-night drivers*. He hopes to find hot rolls, in the warm oven, or better still croissants. Weren't croissants the food for lovers? He thinks that they are. The box of specially chosen cakes will be for a later occasion, a special occasion, easily imagined, and accompanied by broad-brimmed hats and light dresses, most likely flowered chiffon, delicate colours the epitome of elegance for his mother and aunt Dalton. For a moment he lingers over their clothes ...

Miss Vales, Emily, is sure to be obstinate about chiffon. Nylon is her choice.

'It's easy, nylon is. You just put nylon through the suds and hang everything over the rail in the bathroom. Dry as toast over night. Ready to wear. No worries.'

But, first, the croissants. He will take them in a clean paper bag to Miss Vales, to Emily. He will surprise her.

Ahead of him, someone, a man is walking very fast. He thinks it will be easy for him to overtake this man. He has, all his life, played the game of trying the catch up with his father. His father's hair, in this repeated idea, is brown as on the day at the edge of the barley, and not white all round his head as it was later.

In this game of catching up, there is no place for any name, for example Horsefly. Simply the man ahead, always beyond his reach, is his father.

The strange thing about walking in the half light is that old, grey, bent men and women wait indefinitely along the misleading edges of the paddocks, and become, on closer inspection, part of the roadside undergrowth.

The man walking ahead disappears. It is as if the orange and blue lights of the road-house have swallowed him.

Dalton looks both ways along the road. It is now deserted. His father's courteous ways accompanied him during his final distress in the hospital. Dalton, pausing, tries not to think of the pale eyes, frightened and close to him, as he sat near the pillow. His father's eyes filled with tears, he told Dalton he was sorry. The tears were not allowed to overflow. Dalton recalls the empty oxygen cylinder and his father's ineffectual fingers moving upwards in an attempt to push away the oxygen mask during the struggle for more air. His father's face seemed to sink, becoming thin and pinched, starved of life, without animation and losing colour, and he was, all at once, unreachable, as he was unreachable now, always ahead along the road, mostly out of sight.

❧

The warmth of the paper bags in his hands recalls, at once, the way in which aunt Dalton would make it her pleasant duty to hover somewhere, supervising the preparation of the coffee, well sweetened and frothing with freshly boiling milk, poured at the last minute from a tiny saucepan which, travelling together with the even tinier egg saucepan, accompanied her on all her journeys. These fragrant rolls and croissants remind him of Paris or Vienna where aunt Dalton, with a small spoon, liked to drip melted chocolate over the croissants.

'Voila!' she would say, 'I have created an unforgettable *pain au chocolat*.'

❧

In spite of all this seeming, at the present time, ridiculous and unrealistic, for Dalton there is a hopeful consolation in that it is likely the man ahead who disappeared so suddenly would know and approve the choice he has so recently made.

In his own way his father, Dalton has to understand, his father lived his life in the only way he could. There was never any question or suggestion that he should give up, walk out, *shoot through*. He would never have walked away. He would never have abandoned his sister or his wife and certainly not his son. His father always looked upon the best in another person, he saw their good intentions. In recalling his father yet once more, Dalton considers that, like his father, Miss Vales might know of and live by certain plain truths. It was as if she might have the wisdom of knowing and even saying that it was, as time passed, unwise to continue to blame parents or neighbours or even oneself. Even someone as apparently empty headed and stupid as Miss Vales might know things like this. It might be possible that, if he listened to her, he would hear and see that in her speech and behaviour she was uttering beneath her platitudes the one great platitude;

'I'd do anything in the world for you. Anything!'

Dalton considers the possibility, that this being the case, she might even understand and like a poem if he read one aloud to her.

LIEBESLIED (Love Song)

Wie soll ich meine Seele halten, dass
sie nicht an deine rührt?...
Doch alles, was uns anrührt, dich und mich,
nimmt uns zusammen wie ein Bogenstrich,
der aus zwei Saiten eine Stimme zieht.

Auf welches Instrument sind wir gespannt?...
O süsses Lied.

How could I keep my soul so that it might
not touch on yours?...
Yet all that touches us, myself and you,
takes us together like a violin bow
that draws a single voice out of two strings.

Upon what instrument have we been strung?...
Sweet is the song.

R. M. RILKE

ABOUT THE AUTHOR

Elizabeth Jolley was born in the industrial Midlands of England in 1923. She moved to Western Australia in 1959 with her husband and three children. She has worked in a variety of occupations and is currently teaching part time at Curtin University of Technology.

Elizabeth Jolley is acclaimed as one of Australia's leading writers and has received an AO, honorary doctorates from WAIT (now Curtin University) and Macquarie University, and the ASAL Gold Medal for her contribution to Australian literature. Australian literary journals and anthologies have published her fiction and poetry which, together with her plays, have been broadcast on British and Australian radio.

She has published four collections of short fiction, a collection of short essays, *Central Mischief*, eleven novels, of which *Mr Scobie's Riddle* and *My Father's Moon* won the *Age* Book of the Year Award, *Milk and Honey* the NSW Premier's Award, *The Well* the Miles Franklin Award, *The Georges' Wife* the National Book Council Banjo Award for fiction, *Cabin Fever* the FAW ANA Literature Award, and *The Sugar Mother* the France–Australia Literary Translation Award, and a novella, *The Orchard Thieves*.